Charles S. Woodruff

Intellectual Freedom

Charles S. Woodruff

Intellectual Freedom

ISBN/EAN: 9783337291334

Printed in Europe, USA, Canada, Australia, Japan

Cover: Foto ©Andreas Hilbeck / pixelio.de

More available books at **www.hansebooks.com**

INTELLECTUAL FREEDOM;

OR,

EMANCIPATION

FROM

MENTAL AND PHYSICAL BONDAGE.

BY

CHARLES S. WOODRUFF, M. D.,

AUTHOR OF "LEGALIZED PROSTITUTION," ETC.

SINCLAIR TOUSEY,

121 NASSAU STREET, N. Y.

AGENT FOR THE AUTHOR.

TO

THE CAUSE OF HUMAN PROGRESS,

RIGHT, TRUTH, AND JUSTICE,

THIS LITTLE WRITING IS SINCERELY

DEDICATED.

PREFACE.

SEEING the many evils which oppress and enslave the people, both black and white, in all sections of our country, a land called free, prompts me to the writing of this volume, hoping thereby to do something towards the amelioration of the wrongs committed by many of our present social and political institutions.

Slavery, in all forms, is a thing of man, not of God; in His wide domains there is room for all to be free and happy. The Birthright of *all* is LIBERTY.

My aim in writing a work of this kind is not so much to review the *past* as it has been, or the present as it is, but rather to set forth the *new*, the *right* and *truth* of living, as glanced from the equitable and just principles of *nature* in all conditions of life, adhering to her unerring laws as my guide, and draw therefrom logical deductions to the clear comprehension of all my readers, thus showing *life* in all its phases, to be *justly freedom*.

C. S. WOODRUFF.

TROY, N. Y., 1863.

CONTENTS.

CHAPTER I.

PAGE.

NATURE AND HER TEACHINGS. 9

CHAPTER II.

FREEDOM AND SLAVERY. 22

CHAPTER III.

SOCIAL SLAVERY. 33

CHAPTER IV.

RELIGIOUS SLAVERY. 54

CHAPTER V.

PHYSICAL SLAVERY. 101

CHAPTER VI.

EPILOGUE TO AMERICA. 117

INTELLECTUAL FREEDOM.

CHAPTER I.

NATURE AND HER TEACHINGS.

In heading this chapter with the above caption, I do so because there is but *one just* standard of *right*, and that is *nature;* for if there is truth in the world it must have been established by the power that created *all* things, as the finite mind cannot conceive of *good* or *right* as emanating from but one source, and that source Deity. God, or those principles of life which we call by the name of God, invisible essences of creation, the powers that originate and unfold life, either *did* or *did not* originate *this* world, and if the force or forces called Deity did originate the earth, he still sustains and controls it : I say that he *did* make it, and does sustain and control it, and presume upon no opposition to the assertion. We have, then, the fact established and admitted that Deity is the *Author* and *Ruler* of the world (earth), and, as such, is *responsible* for all its attributes, out of which flow all goodness, all truth, all life; therefore do I again back myself up with the assertion that *nature*, fresh from the hands of Deity, is the only *just* standard of *right*, and our

1*

only truthful instructor.   If *in* nature is the *all* of life, and the controller *is* the *omnipotent power*, then it is self-evident that man's source of knowledge must necessarily be in discovering her laws and learning her secrets, since her laws are Deity's instructions, and her secrets his wishes; so that man becomes a truthful teacher only in so far as he unravels and expounds the science of nature, elucidating her laws and principles *justly.* *All of art is nature's *imitation*, all of science her *study*.

I use the word nature in its most comprehensive sense, meaning all of *this*, our globe, *with its productions* and surroundings; while by universe I intend to convey an idea of the *whole* of *creation*, comprising all worlds, all space, all life, as filling, so far as the human mind can conceive, immeasurable immensity; therefore, when I say nature, I mean earth more especially, with *every thing* that pertains thereto; its laws of life, all its different unfoldments, its science, beauty, order, and sublimity, which qualities are unfolded to us by study and culture.   Nature is not an unfathomable mystery, but rather stands ever ready to yield up her truths and treasures to the deserving investigator; as fast as man fits himself by *right culture* to receive, she instructs him nobly and wisely, infilling and enlarging his mental capacity into fulness, that he may really be deserving the place he naturally occupies as the climax of *creative wisdom*, and be capable of solving all the secrets of the natural world, *to* which he belongs, and whose science he should be master of in almost unlimited abundance.

Nature has three kingdoms, or general grades of development, not distinctly separate from each other, but belonging to and sustaining each other *reciprocally*, the basic one of the three being the mineral, next in order the vegetable, then the animal, each sustained by spirit, *ind*welling in its every particle as the *law* of its existence, that spirit or law being Deific vitality, infilling and *causing* earth, life, beauty, and power; bound into all the rest of creation, the same as a cup of water from the ocean is but a small portion of a great sea of water, and separated into the cup from the general fund is still water, the same as man's spirit, separated from the great fund of infinity, is still, in the *individualized* condition, but a portion, a *speck*, of the Deity fund or life element, gradually grown and incarcerated in the physical form for a while, that the physical may be used to good physical purposes, and the spirit *identified* into *personified* intelligence, to find its home in the blue ether,—its native and proper element,—when the physical is laid aside, retaining still its individual power and identity.

The mineral is no more of nature than the vegetable and animal, for *from* the mineral do the vegetable and animal spring: each and all alike products from the maternal womb of nature, and bound in one united whole by the laws of reciprocal unity.

Man in *his* higher state of development belongs to, and depends quite as much upon the forces in the natural world about him for life and sustenance, as the meanest reptile that crawls, or the crudest plant, and owes the same allegiance to the divine laws or

control as the majestic woods and fruitful fields that
everywhere surround him, teeming with life and
beauty. Thus we see the proper relations man sustains to the natural world, and to try to go outside of,
or away from those relations, is to try to go away from
self, since that self is itself a *part* of *nature;* therefore,
to deny one's lord and master, by disowning connec-
tion with and dependence upon the infinitely consti-
tuted authority of bountiful nature, is sacrilege. Man
cannot go *away* from nature because he cannot go
where *nothing is;* if he could leave all other things,
still *himself* would follow and be with him, and constantly under the guide and sustenance of the laws of
his nature.

Trained and brought up under the influence of superstitious customs and beliefs, instead of science,
man learns to regard his being upon earth as a miracle,
from which he finally escapes through miraculous
resurrection at the judgment-day, when the horn of the
man Gabriel shall sound the alarm! A very nice
theory, *if* man had not a reason and common sense to
tell him of a better one, more founded upon *truth* and
natural philosophy; but having wrong training, man
comes to regard the nature, in the midst of which he
is placed and from which he is a germ, as bearing no
relations to him any farther than it serves his comfort
and happiness; he loses, or never gains sight of, the
beautiful relations he sustains to the nature that is so
lavish for his support and advancement, nor once thinks
to catechize her for wise and instructive lessons of life,
while *really* every breath he draws, every enjoyment

and knowledge he gains, is from her vast storehouse, and *he* the *climax* of her wisely working laws for the evolution of the useful, beautiful, intelligent, and refined. Noble man is nature's culmination in the progress of development and unfolding of her vast riches and mighty secrets, for man *is* her profoundest secret; he stands the crowning result of those beautiful and wonderful operations of nature, which, for an illimitable time, have been working his magical evolution, and yet he forgets to turn from his grand stand-point in the advance, and note the series of growths and gradations of unfoldment by which he has attained to his present development, knowledge, and usefulness; forgets to study the scientific laws, through whose operation he has a being, and is sustained in his proper sphere; forgets that *to* nature he owes every thing, and *from* her must gain all his life, growth, knowledge, and wisdom.

Nature is *all* alive; man her highest development and most wonderful and powerful production; eternal progress is her aim, and incessant ACTION her secret of richness and beauty. Change continual and everlasting marks her onward march. The *present*, like the to-days, is fast becoming *yesterdays*, while the new is ever coming like the to-morrow, so steady, sure, and perfect does the passage of time work its unfoldings, adding each moment a drop to the eternity of the *past*, and drawing constantly one atom more from the inexhaustible *future*. We see the old die, and note the changes which follow in the new springing life therefrom, and exclaim, Surely *death* is *life*, and change progress! The world constantly dies to live, and lives to die, and, watching her processes, we learn that were *death* not, *life* could not be. Thus is *every thing* life, and *death* only the *change* it undergoes to better live. Death is a comparative term, and means simply a change of *action*, change of shape and mission, the *decomposed* matter living as much and really in its decomposition as before, decomposing being a step in its refinement.

Creation is a unit, and yet composed of innumerable units, all in unity or harmony of action, all *at-one*, and *life* is self-sustaining. The forces of nature all act in spheres or spherically, the chain of action being an eternal round; there is no end, so far as we can conceive, and consequently there could have been no beginning to life; it always has been, *is*, and ever will be, and perpetual motion is its eternal order.

Of atoms or worlds the *form* is *round*, a single cell constituting vegetable or animal fibre, being as complete as a world. All nature is but a vast conglomeration of minute cells, or in other words *microscopic worlds*, in which indwells the spirit of life, giving each one affinity and usefulness with all the rest. Thus we analyze matter by reducing it to the very finest conditions which material means are capable of doing, and ascertain that there is no end to its divisibility; however fine, it still is matter possessed of life, the same as before its trituration, and by the nicest means found in the chemist's laboratory, the exact point where *matter leaves off* and *spirit begins*, has never been ascertained, neither can it ever be, and he who labors to draw a *dividing* line must ever labor in vain, there being such mutual relations and blendings between them as will not admit of separation.

Matter is the *crudest spirit; spirit* the most refined and attenuated *matter.* Matter *is not*, without spirit, and spirit is not, without matter; they hold opposite *extremes*, the beautiful *mean* being man's *brain matter.* Could we conceive of the possibility of the separation of spirit from matter, we could understand such a thing as annihilation—neither can be. Like *good* and *evil*, matter and spirit bear comparative relations to each other, both one and the same in opposite extremes, yet ever in the *mean* blending beautifully. Earth is continually imbued and vitalized by spirit penetrating every portion of it, animate and inanimate, which grows the grass-blade, sustains animal life, works out its own science through its own productions, and, being comparatively as much in man as in other forms of life, dwells as much *with* him as a thousand miles in air; so *earth* and *heaven* are eternally together, the same as matter and spirit, the terms being identical, earth and matter, heaven and spirit. I speak not of the fabulous heaven of superstitious dogmas, *material* and paved with *gold*, where congregate the resurrected *material bodies*, but of the *true* heaven where dwell *disembodied* souls, and which bears the same relation to *earth* as does spirit to matter; for it would hardly be logical to say that spirits dwell in material abodes—material in the sense of *crude*, unspiritualized matter—but more in accordance with science, philosophy, and good sense, to give them habitation in the blue ether, which surrounds earth, and is the spirit element of nature, or *spiritualized* element of nature. Heaven *ind*wells in the human soul, and that soul, whether clothed upon by the mortal or immortal, is continually in heaven *if* serving the high and useful mission of *living out* the object of its creation.

In a creation which finite minds cannot determine any bounds, beginning or end to, by any known laws of life, does the idea of a *located* heaven, *fenced* in, in the *unknown somewhere*, seem reasonable or logical? Creation, on the contrary, is all wrapped up within itself, matter and spirit continually, beautifully blended together ; and the *earth*, with all the other worlds and systems of worlds of which we know something through astronomical science, and the vast amount which we are unable to fathom, constitute *creation*, all God, all nature, all life, matter, and spirit. It is all one beautiful *whole*, too grand for the human mind to fully contemplate, and too extended for its circumscription or centralization.

We are the legitimate offspring of *this* portion of creation, earth, and as such it is our *first* duty to know something of the source from whence we spring, the nature that surrounds us, and of which we form a part. *Self*-study and the study of nature constitute a momentous task, as pleasing as they are instructive, for they teach us *truth*, which is wisdom ; experience begets knowledge, knowledge wisdom, therefore, ask and it shall be told you, knock and the secrets of nature shall be opened unto you, that you may enter into the enjoyment of all the blessings prepared for those who rightly understand *how* and *why* they live.

As all *truth* is embodied in nature, so all knowledge must be gained therefrom ; there is no other source or fountain to draw from, and those who have the best conceptions of natural laws and forces, will be the most substantial and brightest lights of the age.

It will be ascertained from my writings, that I believe God to be a principle universal, and *not* a personal being, and that that principle is *spirit*, as broad in its application as creation, and that spirit, *life*, and that life *dual*, having, under all circumstances and in all conditions of development, two extremes, or *positive* and *negative* relations, which, blending and balancing, produce the perfect equilibrium there is among natural forces, to rightly understand which, we have to place our conceptions into *terms* of *definite* significance, the same as in speaking of other objects ; therefore, I shall call them magnetism and electricity, magnetism being the positive, or heat, and electricity the negative, or cold ; or magnetism one extreme, and electricity the other, *continually* blending in all things, forming the facts and phenomena of LIFE.

God, then, is a comprehensive *term*, meaning the *whole life* force of *creation*, and the *superstition* connected with the word *God*—the result of ignorance—must give way to the light of science, philosophy, and reason, for the *growing* intellect of man begins to analyze the *subject of life by reason*, rather than longer

believe every mythy theory upon faith alone; faith
is an essential element or faculty of our composition,
but unless under the guidance of *reason*, is often a
hindrance to our progress, leading to the entertain-
ment of wrong beliefs, thus clogging the wheels of
time, whose continual revolutions evolve progression
to the *thinker*.

Life is ours, continually staring us in the face, and
is for us to deal with practically, understanding it
rightly; and living it out *truthfully*. We must first
know *what* it is, then we can give it its right application. It is not something to ever be feared, and
dreamed of, a fancy-painted heaven or hell, but is
with us each moment of *time ;* we act it, breathe it,
consume it, and *live* it constantly; therefore how important we should understand it, and live well and
usefully the *everliving* PRESENT. As the passage of
time is continual, so is the passage of life with us ; a
moment past is a moment gone forever, and ill or well
spent, so eternally remains.

In living, then, we have to deal with facts, science,
and reason, understanding that earth is a part of the
universe, and that *man* is one of its productions, a
microscopic speck, springing into life through *natural*
processes, and roaming awhile upon its surface to do
his mission in life, finally *dissolving* back again into
atomic particles, his spirit, which the body served to
grow, evaporating into air, a spirit entity *as much at
home in its ethereal element* as is the *dust of the body
in earth.*

The ball from whence man springs is his school of

life, and *from* that school must he draw his fill continually; *but he draws as he understands.* Look at a glass globe filled with water and fishes, and you have some faint symbol of the great *sea* of *life*, in which float all the worlds of *immensity;* some slight idea may thus be gained of the universe. Each one of the worlds thus floating in spirit, gives off its own peculiar atmosphere, or spirit emanations. Viewed in this light, let us take the earth, of which we know something, because a part of, swimming as it is in the ether surrounding it, and giving off its own sphere of air and *life* products, from the lowest form of vegetable to noblest man, and then we can form a just idea of the legitimate relations *man* bears to the world from which he originates; he belongs to *earth*, it is *his* native element, and the life forces *in* him and surrounding him, are the means at his command by which he is at will to work out his mission *nobly* or *poorly.* Let him *think* and interrogate nature constantly, and wise and elevated will be his course through the *time* allotted him to live in the clayey tenement, and progressed his entrance into spirit life.

I labor to impress upon the minds of my readers this one idea, that *man* is *born* of *nature*, through the working of natural laws, or forces, and that he must ever turn to her as a child to its mother's breast, to learn his truthful and wise lessons of life.

The nature implanted in man is the *highest development* of the God-powers, and as such, must develop *its own inherent properties irrespective* of the outside world, for there is no parallel to his own being in creation, by which he can shape his course so as to attain the highest perfection; his *own nature*, therefore, must be *worked out* by its own *inherent powers*, and his faculties brought thus to their fullest cultivation; it is his *life science* to do this; the extent of the *capacity* within him to *growth* he but little understands, because the prevailing methods of education are so false to nature's standard, viz.: spontaneous *out*growth rather than labored *in*growth or *instuffing*, that he becomes filled with many erroneous inculcations, to the exclusion of those inceptive truths which are inherent in his nature, and would come beautifully forth, if not choked and crushed by too much *instuffing*.

This is why great men are great, because the nature in them is strong enough to override all wrong educational bias, and the life-forces spring forth to the admiration of the world; oftentimes, too, does the force of circumstances call out the inherent powers, and thus thrust greatness of ideas upon a man. The greatness of an idea is its originality, and the origin of all new things with *man* is simply its discovery; or, in other words, the advanced perceptions of an individual, making discoveries ahead of others of his fellow-beings. The tendency of all human beings is *towards* greatness naturally, that is, progress in development, and increase of perception and understanding. We speak of the enlightenment of the age; true, it is comparatively so, yet "there are more things in earth and heaven than the human mind has ever dreamed of." The enlightenment of the age, as much as it is, is still, comparatively, nothing to what there is to be learned, and *nature* is the *vast storehouse* that holds it all. Man, as yet, knows but little of *himself* even.; his resources and powers are more susceptible of development and more mighty than he knows for; neither can he ever know fully the ultimate of his progress, yet he comes nearest to it when heeding most strictly the laws of his own *interior* nature.

The teachings of nature in every phenomenon of the physical world are very instructive, when we learn to view them through a well-cultivated understanding of her laws, but when viewed from a superficial exterior growth of *ourselves*, learn us but little.

To appreciate nature, we must *first* become her simple, humble, and thorough students; she is *vast* in knowledge and power; her realms the illimitable universe, and her inexhaustible science, God himself. She speaks the voice of her Creator in every manifestation of growth and decay, and man, springing from her maternal womb, must listen, in every act of his life, to the "still small voice" that within *him* is, as a part of the creation, if he would be noble, pure, and wise. *From* nature does he grow, and *to* nature and nature's God is he accountable, and that accountability is *through himself*. *Self*, placed aright, by the proper cultivation, receives the blessing of "well done, thou good and faithful servant" to the *powers of growth within self*.

CHAPTER II.

FREEDOM AND SLAVERY.

In the preceding chapter I have endeavored to show that nature is the source from whence springs man, and his *proper* relations thereto; having done which, I now proceed to the consideration of the *terms, freedom* and *slavery,* designing to speak of them in their absolute and relative conditions. To give force to what I say, I shall aim to set forth my views in a logical and sequent manner, maintaining constantly my dependence upon natural laws; therefore, I shall first notice the *universal* order of creation, and the *mutual* relations the heavenly bodies sustain towards each other, for if there is truth, order, science, and law it. must be among the *infinitely* regulated solar systems, whose perfect harmony of action is *eternally complete.*

So far as man comprehends the vast creations of the Infinite, he does so by means of that little divine spark of life within himself, which he calls his mind or spirit, and which is a *particle* of the God force in nature embodied in his physical organism for a time, probationary to the evolvement of a matured spirit—earth matured. He comprehends, by means of this intelligent *little,* much of the laws that govern the universe, the relations to some extent of mind and matter, and the order and science of the immortal principle of life.

There is no human mind so infinite in its scope of perception as to determine the bounds—if there be any—of creation, and consequently no *centre*. Yet, reasoning from the small to the great, from the known to the unknown, by the metaphysical powers of thought, the only conclusion arrived at is, that there must be a *centre* of power, which originally gave birth to worlds and constellations, and is still the source or fountain-head of infinite life, keeping the order of the universe complete. However true or untrue such reasoning may be, there still remains the unsatisfactory thought, that man cannot fathom divine depths and arrive at the first great *cause* of creation, for man would then be a God, with infinite perceptions; back of his most penetrating and deepest thought remain *unfathomable depths*, and he is obliged to satisfy himself with the point of development to which he has attained, and await the slow processes of *time* to reveal more to his enlarged perceptions.

He can only say that there *is*, from what he sees and knows, an all-sustaining and ruling power, which *he* calls God, and that the order of this ruling power is most perfect and just; that harmony and unity of action mark all universal laws so far as *he* can perceive, and that all things hold MUTUAL relations towards each other. He looks into the science of astronomy, and sees the family of the heavens in most perfect obedience to the laws of *mutual* attraction and repulsion, and this leads him to the consideration that *two* forces, mighty and all-pervading, act to sustain and control the relation of all things to all other things, and these forces he can only determine as *positive* and *negative,* or a power of *drawing* and repelling, a male principle and female principle forming *perfect wedlock,* out of which is borned the useful, the beautiful, the harmony, order, majesty, and sublimity, durability, worth, and progress of creation, *attributes* and *essentials* all of the *infinite;* in short, the *infinite* would become *finite* were it not *perfection;* perfection, not in the sense of having arrived at a point beyond which there is no growth, but perfection in order and progress of growth.

This power of relation between systems of worlds, and orbs to their central orb, can be traced down through all things to the very atom, where still the positive and negative forces hold sway, giving *existence to* the atom by their *mutual* blending; thus from spirit is formed the atom; from atoms, massive worlds; from worlds, constellations; from constellations a universe; and so on till where the end is, man knows not; but from atoms to worlds, and worlds to a universe, the laws of attraction and repulsion, or, in other words, harmony and order, hold good. The *mutual* relations are perfect in the order of economy divine, and *orbs* or *atoms* fulfil the mission assigned by the Creator, teaching man, the acme of embodied intelligence, instructive and useful lessons.

All worlds bear relations of mutual interest to all other worlds, and all things and beings of a world, their inevitable dependence upon and destiny with that world, and thus the laws of creation are as vast as eternal, linked in perfect sympathy of operation, all free and all bond. And so it is the terms freedom and slavery are defined; there is no *absolute* freedom or slavery, but freedom is the MUTUAL relations and dependence of all things to all other things, while *absolute* freedom, or entire and isolated *independence* of all other objects, is impossible. In *one* sense every thing is free; in another and equally truthful sense, every thing is slave, or there is no entire indepen dence, and consequently there is a degree of slavery that is just, *divinely just.*

Thus we see the proper and beautiful relations which all natural powers sustain towards each other, and can deduce therefrom our truthful lessons of life. We learn that man, like all else, is free and slave— free to follow out the laws of *his own* being in their just relations to the world of life about him, and slave only in the laws of *reciprocity*, which demand that he shall give as he receives, and receive as he gives, or that his slavery and freedom shall be of *mutual* dependence.

Absolute freedom, and absolute slavery, I repeat, are impossible; the nearest man can come to the former, is in adhering *strictly* to the higher laws of his nature, while the most absolute slavery consists in being deprived of the full exercise of those higher laws, by taking away, temporarily, the right to use his own body and mind for his highest and best good—the inalienable right vouchsafed to him by his Creator.

2

The justness of divine wisdom is seen in the laws of the universe, holding suns and worlds in reciprocal relations, the power of one being fully reciprocated by another, the sun, or centre of attraction, holding the lesser orbs that revolve about it, with only that degree of power that they in turn exert upon it; the earth, for instance, holds just that amount of attraction for the sun that the sun exerts upon the earth, thereby keeping the harmony, out of which results all the beautiful and useful there is in nature. Herein we learn another law of life, that the strong control the weak, or the larger the lesser, but *only* under *reciprocal* relations, or the controlling power *receiving* only as it *gives;* and most beautiful and instructive is the contemplation of the order divine, as seen in universal laws; and when *man* learns to comprehend those laws, and apply them to himself, will he meet the demands of divine justice *within* himself, knowing the powers of his own being, and *how* to rightly use them. The laws of life are plain, and all that man has to do to rear himself a noble and wise being, is to study into and understand them; they teach him the *right* course in all his dealings, and under all circumstances. Freedom he can only have in its fullest sense by knowing and living up to the laws of his nature. There is no standard of right but the divine, and that teaches plainly that all men are born free, in their reciprocal relations, and that no man has the *God-given* right to call them slaves. What is one man's freedom may be another's slavery, the conditions of humanity are so various; yet what each is capable of enjoying, that is his eternal inheritance, and high or low states of development are attended respectively with their peculiar receptive and enjoyable capacities.

Freedom to the low-born is as much *his* happiness as freedom to the high-born, though the two conditions are widely different; and one is as much accountable to the laws of his being as the other, for as there are not, nor can be any two human developments exactly alike in point of organization, there needs must be every conceivable difference in growth to fill the eternal plan, and form the consecutive links in the great humanitary chain. Such is God's order; and because to keep that order complete there are such varied conditions, man cannot safely infringe upon his weaker brother's rights, nor trespass upon law divine—the elements of truth, light, and life will not admit of it, and monarchies built upon slavery, republics harboring it within the sacred folds of freedom's banner, must ultimately shake and convulse with the mighty throes of revolution to rid themselves of the noxious element, as America is now doing, because it has nursed the adder of slavery, *mental* and physical, at its national breasts, fed the many-tongued viper from its own warm blood, until at last it turns and stings her to the heart; and behold her mighty agony in administering the antidote— horrid *civil* war!

The just relations between the high and low born— I use the terms high and low in the sense of development, not blood—should ever be determined by the divine standard of right, as seen regulating in harmo-

ny all things, and no man be another's slave or master
any further than he gives as he receives, and *vice
versâ.* For one man to deprive another of the free use
of his powers of life is grossly wrong, I care not how
low in the scale of development he may be. Even the
brute should be the recipient of humane and kind care,
for the service he brings us; the law of reciprocal inter
est should extend to the horse or ox, and he be given
all he can receive in food and kindness for his use to
man. Under *all* circumstances there stands the law
of reciprocity, to try and evade which, brings a sure
penalty.

Slave is a word not written in the divine voca-
bulary, save that which confers a mutual benefit;
there is no such thing any where in the broad universe
as slavery or oppression, sanctioned by right divine,
but on the contrary, every language of the Omnipotent, as written in every science and upon every
natural outburst of life power, teaches that all things
are *free.*

Man transgresses the laws of life and penalties follow, which is most emphatically exemplified in the
mighty tumult which upheaves and dismembers our
fair land of America—"the land of the *free* and
home of the brave," and likewise the land of the
slave! She but pays the penalty of her misdeeds; in
her heart's core, the Constitution, has she nursed the
seedlings of slavery, vile and corrupting to every thing
it touches, until it has grown to a gigantic size,
almost outvieing in power the very principles of freedom; law divine has been transgressed and the conse-

quences follow, and terible must be her punishment, for grave have been her errors. No power can intervene to stay the revolution, bloody and terrible as it is, until her regeneration is complete, and the full penalty of her wrongs given ; for the law of reciprocity is one of supreme justice, and no hand can stay its avenging power until right is made might. The era of *reason* and *justice* dawns, and in proportion to its advance must fall off the shackles of *error* and *superstition*. Oppression of the low born has been in our midst, oppression of free thought and free speech, oppression of *mind* to *ignorance* and *priestly craft*, to *fashion* and *form*, and a thousand vices of living, the result in a very great degree of wrong education, a passion rule, gratifying morbid tastes and desires, selfish greediness and animal propensities, and now stern justice is striking her axe, with masterly power and skill, at the root of the monster evils, that the divine fiat may be executed, which went forth in the construction of the world. America set herself up to be a free nation, after hard struggles to free herself from the despotic tyranny of aristocratic Europe, planting herself upon the God-given principles of *liberty*, and *immediately* began suckling at her maternal breast an institution of slavery, which gradually worked its way securely into the national heart as one of the rights of its Constitution, and the result of two diametrically opposed institutions, freedom and slavery, is at hand, and we are fighting again the bloody battles of the revolution, but this time to free ourselves of the accursed· institution we ourselves

have reared in our midst, through short-sighted and
temporal views; this time however, ten-fold more des-
perate because more powerful, and thrice horrible because a *civil* strife.

Nations, like individuals, must pay the penalty of
wrong doing, and always revolutions occur as the natural result of disobeying divine justice. The blood-
shed and carnage, the wails of bereaved thousands, that
desolate our fair land and make sad the hearts and
hopes of all, cannot be averted, for the *causes* have
been aggravated, and while they last the *effects* must
be seen and felt. It is a sad thought however, that
many who have lived entirely innocent of the dark
stains which are now being wiped out, should bear
part of the burden of dire war, and share in suffering
its calamities, yet in the common lot of a nation's
people, the innocent must suffer ofttimes for the
guilty; yet there is a consolation in knowing, that
out of all our sufferings will eventually come the
brightest nation, the grandest republic the world ever
saw. Purged and cleansed of all our national sins
we shall stand forth a most glorious example of
human liberty, based upon the God-given principles
of freedom. America takes the lead among nations,
the beacon light for the world to follow; Europe
trembles upon the verge of revolution, and monarchies and aristocracies seem crumbling beneath the
light of increasing *justice* and the advance march of
truth. And why should it not be so? If there is a
power supreme, sitting in judgment over all temporal and eternal things, and that power is a just

God—a divine principle of life, from whose almighty and inexhaustible fountain spring all worlds, all life, all truth and justice, it must eventually bring under subjugation *to* divine rule the wayward and erroneous actions of *man*. Either man is more mighty than Deity or that Deity is not just, *if* man is *not* brought to the acknowledgment of the *right*, and governed by eternal principles. As he grows to the better exercise of reason, he must yield obedience to the laws which govern him as an *individual*, and being and doing right as *individuals*, *nations* will not go astray from just action.

Man cannot deal in wrongdoing and prosper in his lasting, eternal progress, though a short lifetime may seem very brilliant in point of ill-gotten worldly gains, yet the *laws* of his life follow him whithersoever he goeth, and sooner or later the judgment is pronounced, from which he can find no escape but the full payment of the penalty. Justice may not overtake him in *this* life, but somewhere the divine demand comes, and he must answer thereto.

The histories of all nations have been scenes of prosperity and revolution, which must still continue to be, until *human laws* act in *harmony* with *divine*, and mankind learn to walk in those paths of rectitude and honor marked out for them in the laws which govern them in common with the universe.

America struggled hard to give birth to the first child of liberty, but the descendants of those noble and patriotic grandsires, who waded through rivers of blood, and battled with and surmounted by almost superhuman efforts mighty obstacles, that we might be free, have forgotten, in our selfish greed after worldly gains, the *principles* of *right* to a very great extent, and the consequence is, that to-day, America is again in the agonies of travail to give birth to the second child of freedom, upon whose broad Atlantean shoulders is to be borne the emblazoned emblem of TRUTH and LIBERTY to the world. The first struggle. was *principle* warring with *outward* oppression; to-day it is principle warring with *internal* wrong, with slaveocracy in its many forms, aristocracy, monopoly, and the hydra-headed monster of evil.

Reforms should commence with marriage, the cradle, and in early life. Man reared aright from his beginning, and he remains so. It is useless to be striking at *effects* while *causes* remain untouched.

We cannot expect the ballot-box to decide with justice, while those, many of them, who cast the votes, know nothing of the first principles of their own beings, and consequently nothing of the principles of divine freedom and right. Long prior to a man's public life, lies the training which fits him for it. In the maternal womb begins his being, and as that beginning is in accordance with the divine laws of procreation, so will be the man, shaped much by training and circumstances in the early years of life. Fundamental to his existence and after career lie the laws of life, and in their *study* and *observance* is to be found the key to all reform. Not in rituals, not in prevailing customs and beliefs, not in the past with its superstitious and barbaric notions, but in the *living present* is the growing reason of man to find the instruments for his use, and instructions for his guidance. No age has been so rife with spiritual knowledge, light, and insight as *this*, and therefore no age with what *has been*, can serve to guide us of the nineteenth century. We are farther progressed upon the great sea of time than any who have gone before, and from the times in which we live must draw the means to meet every emergency of our lives; must "take time by the forelock," and make ourselves masters of our own conditions. Times of prosperity develop the *commercial* resources of a country; times of war its *mental* capacities.

Put at the helm of the "ship of state" men of right knowledge and principles, to execute just laws, and she will sail on smooth seas of peace and prosperity.

Long prior to man's appearance the divine edict went forth, and it must be heeded; the cause of humanity, freedom, love, justice, and truth demand its observance.

CHAPTER III.

SOCIAL SLAVERY.

PRIOR to every thing physical is the spiritual, for the spirit is the *cause* of material existence; in other words, the *principle* of *life*, or God, *was* before the physical world had being. The *infinite* reared the *finite*, that is, the first great *cause operated* and worlds

2*

and a universe were born. The terms *infinite* and finite are *comparative* terms, and here used as such; but strictly speaking, every thing is *infinite*, and *finite* pertains to those things and forms of being, like man's physical form, which rapidly *change*, suffering, at the option of infinite law, rapid and frequent metamorphoses. The finite to us is the tangible world about us, which we can grasp, measure, weigh, and thus comprehend; the infinite, that which is unfathomable by man of the creation, arriving at ultimate causes. The world in which we live, and which is to us tangible, and we ourselves, are but *parts* of the infinite, all having life breathed into them by the infinite, eternal, life-giving principle called God by us, and by different nations different names. Matter, merely as such, has no life without spirit, or the tangible, immediate material is *inseparably* allied to the infinite, dependent wholly thereupon. Of all creation, *God* is the *cause*, God is *spirit, spirit is the life;* consequently, as the *spirit* is, so is the condition of the material it gives life or being to; therefore, in understanding the *spiritual* lies the power to properly control the *physical*. Spirit is the *cause*, matter the *effect*, intimately, inseparably, and eternally blended. Man is not an exception to the general laws of birth, growth and life, as seen in the physical world about him; the same laws that pervade the universe, pervade also and control him, and in their study lies his highest good, for he can no better seek to know the proper uses and purposes of his being, than by learning the *causes* which continually operate to control him; going to the fountain source, and tracing the cause and effect of his existence, all the way up from the beginning to full manhood, then stands he forth before the world a man of knowledge, power and wisdom, because *knowing self*. He understands himself according to the higher principles of his nature, and is ever prepared to act under all circumstances, readily, justly, and wisely, for he knows the *right* and follows therein ; he has accomplished the first duty and study of his life, in learning the *right use of self*. Such is truly an educated man, though he may never have seen the inside of a school-house or college ; may not have read Virgil, Butler, or any of the great authors, yet be a scholar, scholastic in the knowledge of *his own powers* of *life* and the *laws* of *nature ;* know *why* he lives, and *how* to live to make his life the success it was given him to make.

What is man, that he should so puff himself up with great pretension ? He cannot outrun nature, and the insects that crawl beneath his feet are wiser than he. The little ant and busy bee build with more of beauty, art, and utility than man, and live in fulfilment of their mission in life, under the guidance of native instinct, better than does man with all his mighty bombast, and pretended skill and knowledge ; yet is man infinitely, almost, the higher development ; but, notwithstanding his great superiority of growth and power, he cannot be wiser than the insect, and in no way its equal in purity and wisdom, save by giving as strict allegiance to the laws of *his nature* as does the insect.

All temporal forms have a beginning ; so man sprang

into life, so far as his mundane existence is concerned, in a very low state of development, and for many ages, through the slow, *consecutive* processes of natural unfoldment, has been gradually rising in the scale of growth, worth, intellect, and God-like powers, until to-day we find him going through the process of developing his reason and intellectuo-spiritual faculties. What his past has been is very easy to discern; for tracing the laws of life, by means of the growing reason, we see that his beginning must, according to all the analogies of nature, have been very crude, and the first outburst of life-power but *one* grade above the brute. His knowledge, like his development, was then more of the brute instinct than of reflection,—a somewhat refined animal instinct. Thus, undoubtedly, for long eras was man growing, subject to the control of his instinct, which led him in purer paths of life than at a far more advanced period of growth, when the enlarged intellect became too strong to be wholly governed *by* instinct, and still not sufficiently developed to come under the control of reason. Thus we trace man from the first stage of *human* existence into the *second*, which seems to have been the age of semi-human barbarity, when the animal instincts were no longer able to wholly control the increased perceptions, nor the intellectual faculties sufficiently enlarged to control the animal propensities, consequently the strife between the two, instinct and intellect, has been manifest in many cruel barbarities of ages long prior to history, undoubtedly, and within the scope, also, of historic recollection.

The divine injunction has been obeyed, however, as an unavoidable fatality, and the progress of the human race been steadily onward, toward higher development, loftier aims, and grander results. Divine justice has stood at the helm, and divine plans been carried forward despite the wayward and angry tendencies of undeveloped man—of man in his transitional state between the brute and human—and although long ages have doubtless rolled past, yet is man but just emerging from his animal tendencies upon planes of high moral and intellectuo-spiritual advancement.

For generations past has man been bursting the bonds of fettered ignorance, and coming slowly upon those planes of development where intellect, pure metaphysical intellect, is beginning to lead him in the paths of his nature—in paths of knowledge and scientific investigation, which unfold to his enlarging perceptions something of the *causes* of his existence, and teach him the laws of his life ; yet, through how much superstition and error he has struggled to arrive at his present growth, the histories of the past, and the mockeries of the present under the garb of religion, can best tell. It is *my* mission to introduce *new* thoughts, and not to rake among the *ruins* of the *past* for ideas, therefore I shall leave my readers to make research and learn for themselves, what they may wish to know of what *has been*. *I* had much rather be engaged in studying the *living present* and gaining revelations therefrom. The *past*, as compared with the *future*, is but little in the eternity of time, through-

out whose endless ages endure all things, and man
cannot grow rapidly while engaged in revoking or
re-enacting the scenes of the past in memory. What
has gone into the oblivion to which *time* consigns all
things, should there be left as having served its purpose, and gone forever from view *as it was*. The order
of life is *change ;* and motion incessant is revolving
and renewing the affairs of the world in ever increasing and progressive action ; as fast as things temporal
serve the purposes for which they were created, so
fast do they pass, or change away, to leave room for
new developments in their stead. Man stands at the
climax of creation, and it is for him to keep pace with
the divine order of existence, and consequently he
should not be dozing over the scenes and superstitions
of the *past ;* time is too precious to be thus wasted,
nor his allotment of it any too long for his perfection,
though *all* be well applied. So long as he is the van-
guard, so to speak, in the processes of development
which all nature is gradually undergoing in its infinite
fatality, he should keep even pace not only with the
changes of time, but in his understanding anticipate
them, and be ever ready to meet with the inception of
more light and truth ; the windows of his soul should
ever be open to the divine influx of knowledge, that
he may with wisdom execute every design of his creation. In this way would man become a free being,
dependent only upon the laws of reciprocal unity, and
ever ready to act according to the higher intuitions of
his expanding nature. *Out* of himself would come
forth the light to guide him aright, and *not* out of the

misconceptions of a sleepy world, sleeping amid the bigotry and superstition of bygone ages, not *daring* to look ahead of the timeworn and stale doctrines of *man*-made creeds and customs. The laws of our beings should be the creeds of our lives, and their *observance* constitute our highest duties and purest worship.

Human mentality was not made to be slave bound to worldly *forms*; every law of life disproves it, yet as we look abroad into the world and note the varied conditions of societies bound up in the observance of popular, wholly *worldly* ceremonies, as meaningless as shallow, not daring to step outside of the customary routine, convinces us how really people are slaves to social customs, while few, indeed, of those who have any higher appreciation of right, dare to live up to their better judgment for *fear* of the *frowns* of *their neighbors—slaves* to the *popular opinion*—nor dare to exercise life in accordance with the fullest capacity of reason—*moral cowards! Mind* makes the man what he is, and if that is not allowed its full exercise, its full scope of action, small indeed becomes its capacity to grasp after and understand any thing outside of its usual routine of thinking; it becomes hemmed in by the continual observance of old staid notions, to the exclusion of progressive ideas, and the acquirement of a riper knowledge of its own powers. Man has now arrived at that stage of development, when the mind will not much longer submit to the shackles of old superstition, imposed by clerical authority, for the bud of human growth is bursting the shell which has so long encased it, and beginning to take a broader and deeper survey of the affairs of life. The increased perceptions are piercing beneath the surface of a false society, crusted over by a fabulous theology. It is the age of philosophy, and *demonstration* takes the place of blind belief; *proof* is needed to satisfy the hungerings of the restless spirit, and *faith* and *outside* show will not much longer hold noble man in "durance vile," for there is an eternal spark within him, which is too much in sympathy with the progressive designs of the *infinite*, to long be held in slavish stupidity to a *worldly* power, which is as false to every beautiful principle of human existence as is hell to heaven ; for where else but to hell would this same worldly power damn you, if you but assail its stronghold, or set reason upon its track ?

Man is a cosmos ; in him all the attributes of the world from which he is formed are found, and he ultimately must be as free as the eternal power formed him. All the rituals and false ceremonies of the social world must soon give way to man's growing reason necessarily, for in proportion to the enlargement of the intellectual faculties, so will be the perceptions, enabling him to look deeper and deeper into the laws of his own existence, unraveling gradually the science of truly and rightly living, and, as a self-adjusting law, work out the axiom of his creation.

In each human being naturally dwell all the attributes of life, and by his or her cultivation are they to be brought forth in good and wise *action*. The responsibility of being all that was designed in our creation rests, in a great measure, with each one ; for the principles of life *indwell* in every faculty of our organisms, like the germ principle in the seed, and it remains for us to *out*grow them by the right and proper pruning and care, so that for all the lack there is in our developments we are to blame, since the forces of nature are ever striving to expand into fullness.

Were it not for so much social slavery, the bondage of mind unto mind, there would be very much more general advancement and enlightenment in the world. The *mind*, I have said, makes the man, consequently unless it is left free to contemplate, to the full extent of its capacity, the science and beauty of nature, thus expanding and educating the brain, it will not grow full and strong, and its development remains imperfect, as its *actions* will show. *Wisdom* is the boon of life which all crave and admire, but wisdom is not the product of a stinted mind—a restricted intellect. *Freedom* is the *magic* that gives to all *action* a *forward impetus*, and develops the deep hidden resources of the human soul. Free action, free *thinking* and free *speech* are *growth;* but overcome, held in slavery, by the *fear* of popular disapprobation, by *moral* cowardice, what are the faculties of the mind good for? Man might as well hinge himself upon some mechanical steam-power and thus go through the world, so far as real growth and worth are concerned. Most people are engaged in talking other people's thoughts, using other's brains and thus chiming in with the common herd.

Every man has a *brain* of *his own*, and that brain

is only highly useful by the constant rubbing and pol-
ishing of *thinking* and *acting* for itself, under all circumstances. Brains are worth nothing save as they
are capable of understanding the science of life, and
giving *demonstrations* thereof in *speech* and *action*.
To educate the young brain is to use such *keys* of
nature as will wind it up so that it will run of *itself*,
and keep time to its *own* construction. Minds that
talk others' minds, and follow in the wake of *their*
opinions, are worth nothing. Man owes himself his
whole attention, giving which his life *outflows* in elevated and wise actions, that are ever a benefit to himself and his fellow-men. He has no responsibility
save to himself, his fellows, and his God, which is *all*
summed up in the strict *observance* of the *laws* of *his
being;* and as every human being is different in
organization from every other, it rests with each to
observe the laws of his or her constitution, *regardless*
of the peculiarities and fallacies of the outside world.
To be a law unto self is clearly the rule of life, that
is : to study and observe the laws of one's own being,
inasmuch as one cannot *act* for another, in the matter
of growing and cultivating the mentality, *out*bringing
the powers *in*herent in human nature. The peculiarities of one mind are not those of another, for the
divine order of creation is not ever rendered monotonous by an exact repetition; but the productions of
nature are as infinite in variety, as the *mind* is *infinite* that gives them existence. No two productions
of man were ever just alike, for the purposes of each
are fulfilled with each, and needs not a second edition;

indeed it would be too near an approach to "old fogyism" in the infinite, to give forth editions of human nature unchanged; while I believe it would be an impossibility from the very laws of creation, which are *progressive*, and must necessarily never produce two organized entities exactly the same; therefore do we see the impossibility of generalizing rules of living, any farther than strict adherence to the *Deific Prinples* of life. Divine law must necessarily be man's order, as *individual distinctness* is the divine rule, as seen in all the phenomena of life. Every manifestation of nature speaks an order divine, to which man must give due regard since he is a product of the *Divine Will*, subject in every respect to the ruling, originating power; though man, being the highest intelligent product of creative wisdom, has therefore the strongest volition, and to some extent may transgress the laws of life, as he most certainly does too often, but always to the injury of himself, and *not* the law. As the growing intellectual faculties expand into greater fulness, giving the perceptive organs deeper insight into the affairs of life, man must come under the guidance of *reason*, which is his most Godlike attribute—the little divinity placed within him to rule his organism in accordance or harmony with the plans *of* the infinite, *so soon* as the intellect perceives those plans. It is said "God's ways are not man's ways," which I do not believe. God's ways must *necessarily* be man's ways, since man can have no ways but by and through the *laws* of his creation, though man may and does try to plan and act for himself inde-

pendently of any knowledge of a higher power, but only
in proportion as his plans are in accordance with the
infinite does he *really* succeed.   Every *seeming*
worldly success is not really such, for upon *material*
things *alone*, has not God placed the highest worth;
material being only the clay, so to speak, which the
spiritual moulds at will, into vessels and instruments
to serve, for a time, the object for which they are
created, but as such, that is vessels and instruments,
they do not remain eternally cognizable, and therefore are not to be eternally relied upon. *Material*
things undergo *continual* metamorphoses at the option
of the *spiritual*. Man is only a vessel, so far as his
physical existence is concerned, to be used for a time
by the *in*dwelling spirit, serving the object of his
creation, and that object the *out*wroughting of this
indwelling intelligence into *truthful* and *useful*
ACTION, which can only be done by the powers of life
enveloped in its own nature. The indwelling life
principle of Mr. A. cannot develop the inherent ener-
gies of Mr. B.'s organism, or make his vessel, or machinery fulfil the object of its creation, and "*vice
versâ;*" but the powers of each are to be *out*wrought
by each separate from the other, or, at least, only
aided by the *mutual* relations they may sustain towards each other. Like the seed that contains the
germ of life for the future plant, and can only be
developed into the kind of plant for which its germ
is designed, so man must learn to look upon himself,
and develop what is *within* him, rather than be try
ing to *fill* himself with what is *out*side—the *rubbish*

of other people's thoughts. The *instuffing* process is not substantial; grander, sublimer depths of man's interior nature must be explored and brought out, to the best good of self and the admiration of the world, to form an enduring basis. The social customs and forms, that now breed so much of slavery of mind and opinion, are soon to be abolished, for man begins to see himself as he *really is*, and to rightly prune and culture that self upon its own just merits—to develop the nature within, with a view to something more permanent than is now afforded by the superficial, gewgaw trappings of an artificial society—superficial in education, thought, reading, dressing, and action.

I have endeavored to set forth, thus far, the divine principles of life as applied to human existence; and having stated my views of the designs and conditions of man's creation, I shall next endeavor to show how well the social world is living out the *divine object* of *human* life, to do which I must necessarily look into the condition of society around me; and, as I gaze and peer with deeply scrutinizing perceptions into the social elements, many are the families I behold who bow industriously to the money god, making themselves slaves to labor, that they may be counted among the votaries of fashion; fashion as established not by *real* worth and upon *truth*, but the fashion of *wealth*, which *apes* at the *aristocracies* of *monarchical Europe;* positions reared with money as their basis, a basis founded upon the ill-gotten millions of the so-called *rich*, for riches *are* ill gotten, that do not compensate the laborer according to just, reciprocal laws. Thus the conditions of actual servitude to the mammoth goddess of dress and fashion, are very various, showing a people actually worshipping mammon to the degree of real physical and mental slavery and imbecility. Great riches are the result of avarice and pure selfishness, that selfishness which monopolizes the common wealth of a country and *starves* the *poor !* for just in proportion as the few become extremely rich, do the masses become poverty-stricken. The wealth of a country is so much, which the population of that country make, and it is mostly made by the labor of the poor, while the few, who happen to have the most brains and the least conscience, and the clearest insight into affairs, make the light they possess the means for grinding out of the poor's labor princely fortunes. Such I hold to be *not* in accordance with divine teaching, but the result of pure animal selfishness.

All human beings are the children of *one* supreme power, and the world is given them to grow from, subsist upon, and enjoy, and is the *common* property of all, which all could and would have plenty of, if it were not for the extreme selfishness of mankind. Were there no such thing as selfishness any farther than to supply the *natural* needs of the body, there would be no vast accumulation of fortunes, and consequently every one would have enough to render them free and happy, and not be obliged to wear life out in enslaving drudgery to compete with a greedy world.

There is no good reason why mankind should not

all be in easy, happy circumstances, and have plenty of time for *self-culture;* but as the conditions of humanity are to-day, money is the controlling power, the great god, the sublime aim of a people calling themselves civilized and enlightened. Ay! enlightened in every thing save the pure *truths* of life and *right* use of self.

The American people bow in humble submission to the behests of mammon, sacrificing their highest and holiest principles at the altar of the almighty dollar, because, forsooth, the *popular* custom is wealth and fashion, which mean, when put in proper language, *sin* and *folly.*

This is where we stand to-day; the more developed of us, those whom the circumstances of time have smiled upon most favorable, are giving loose rein to the selfish propensities, grasping, monopolizing, and using the riches of the land for our own lofty worldly aggrandizement and power, making slaves of the masses, and ourselves slaves to a foolish pride, slaves to a *material* power, which brings luxury and dissipation to the body, and long, lasting curses to the soul. Upon this *wealth* basis is the social code reared and its institutions founded, and how well the devotees of fashion are submitting to the slavery imposed by mammon, the struggles and throes, discontents and inharmonies which pervade societies, and the consequent laws and prisons, asylums and poor-houses, sustained in their midst, will best tell.

With our present state of society, man becomes a constant slave to almost superhuman toil to meet the demands, which the expenses of supporting a family *in style* make upon him, and then must often sacrifice principle and honor to compete with the greedy world about him for gain. So long as the standard of worth is wealth, every manner of living must correspond.

With a land overflowing, in times of peace, with plenty of every thing for man's material wants, and adorned with the beautiful for the elevation and enlivening of his soul, yet are the beauties and grandeurs of nature, with their teachings and exhilarating influences, little cared for by man in his low aims. And through the power of wealth in the hands of the few, provisions range, considering their plenty, at very high prices, so that the poor find starvation at times actually staring them in the face! Oh, in such a land as America, with a people calling themselves free, that there should be such a condition as *poor people !*

Sending millions and millions of dollars' worth of our country's products every year to foreign ports, taking in exchange gaudy foreign manufactures wherewith to deck and adorn richly the body, while there are *poor* at home actually starving!

Oh, American People! what must be the sins to atone for when time shall have stricken off the mortal coil, and with it the shackles of ignorance and superstition, and you are brought before that eternal tribunal of stern justice, which *all* must soon face!

It is time strong language was used—*truth* is always strong—in speaking of the evils of the present time, which underlie the business and social world, for, as a people, we are fast going into physical and moral degeneracy. The houses of refuge, prisons, insane retreats, and dens of ill fame, speak more against our manner of living, than the pen can do; for the requirements of the social world, with its extravagance, power, artificialities, and hypocrisies, drive very many, through the commitment of penal offences and otherwise, into these very places, as the only hiding-places from the scorn and persecutions of an uncharitable, *Christian* (!) state of society.

Christ is looked to as an example of purity, charity, and right worthy our highest imitations, but, alas! only *looked to*, *not* imitated, and *he* had not where to lay his head that he could call his own; no princely palace in which to dwell in high pomp and dignity, and from which to condescend to give *occasionally* a few paltry coppers to the poor, but ever sought the *lowly*, to give them words of cheer and instruction, making himself as *one* of *them*, and overthrowing the tables of the *money-changers* in the temple, a rebuke against such proceedings, which might well be re-peated at the present time *in America*. Yet this same *act* of Jesus is preached upon often from the *sacred* (!) desk to listening thousands, but never *acted* upon, save it be by a solitary individual or two. Can we find any better example than that which Christ set us? *if not*, why not live it out in our every-day affairs? Simply because our social systems are found-ed upon a wrong basis,—a *wealth* basis instead of *principle;* and it requires that a man should be some-what avaricious, however repugnant it may be to his better sense, to live with a grasping, selfish world,

3

where even the *wealthy* often cheat and defraud the *starving poor* for a paltry *dollar* or two, as I have often known. Such things, and conditions of living must be eradicated, for there is a power over that of man's whose ways are those of *principle* and *justice*, and the inception of whose truths must eventually emancipate the world from all wrongs, placing humanity upon planes of *charitable* brotherhood.

I know well, that reforms cannot be instantaneous, and that the prevailing customs of a time oblige many to resort to expediencies of business dishonorable, rather suffer the stings of pride or starve, but I know, too, that the inevitable tendency of the *higher* laws is towards man's enlightenment and *true* civilization; therefore does it become my duty to plant some of the seeds of reform, that they may be taking root for *future*, if not present good.

The principles of divine justice are the " leaven in the meal," which must eventually leaven the whole human family, for I see it is rapidly working, and through those whose perceptions are deepest and clearest must these principles be evolved to the understanding of the multitude. The bonds of ignorance which now rivet the social world with the manacles of false pride and error, must be severed, and the inception of light and truth, make all hearts glad and *free*. The wrongs of society must gradually be emancipated, as now the turmoil and strife of a nation in civil conflict is *surely* doing. Reforms come with and without wars, but the greatest reformation occasioned by any war is now being enacted upon our own continent; America pours out her blood freely to wash away the dark sins of a nation, deep rooted and wide spread throughout her fair land. The South has crimsoned her hands and stained her honor with the ominous gore of Africa's sons and daughters for nearly a century, and the North, calling *herself free* has nursed around her hearthstones and in her public sanctuaries, bigoted and aristocratic notions in imitation of monarchical Europe, and run mad over her easily-gotten gains. The *causes* of war have been aggravated and the reformation will be great. The rotten institutions of both sections must crumble before the invading monarch of stern justice, and the social fabric be reared upon *Principle* instead of wealth.

Gold, as a medium of business is valuable, but placed upon its right basis, is of no more value than the things it buys—is a mere metal, and worshipped, leads the mind *down* rather than *up*—having no more intrinsic worth than other metals; and in proportion as it is set up as a god, and bowed unto, just in that ratio do people become idolaters and unprincipled rogues, for its very worship involves the *sacrifice* of *principle*. Gold, given its just value, as compared with the material world becomes plenty, and every thing of daily need, cheap. It is the *money-changers* of our own time, and *speculators*, who give such an undue value to it, by their dishonest and selfish graspings. Such things are on a par with highway robbery, and such men, viewed in the light of *principle*, no better than robbers, for they steal and

hoard away the common riches of the country, to an
extent that does not *naturally* belong to them, and,
by so doing, literally defraud many of their just
share. Such men infest every community, and are
the curses which bereave a nation's people, causing
many poor, miserable, half-starved paupers in the
land. If the riches of the country were not thus
hoarded away into coffers, by a set of vampires, and
moneyed bloodsuckers, there would be a great plenty
for all, and every man be rich.

The social world is in worse thraldom to wealth and
fashion to-day, than is the African with the chains of
physical servitude clanking upon his feet. This great
love of money is the giant evil that stalks in so many
different shapes over our beautiful land, and blights
with its foul touch so many happy homes and hearts.

That there is *truth* in the assertions I make, every
one who has any perception whatever must know;
while those who have been all their lives slaves to surrounding circumstances, will feel the force of my re-
marks, and concede them true, from a knowledge which
is *practical* within themselves. What I write for is, to
see society placed upon its right basis, to see principles,
not dollars, its code of honor; I would see every one
free, rich, and happy, and none bowed down in abject
poverty, because the riches that should in part belong
to them, are stolen away by the few; I would see man
in his proper sphere in life, fulfilling the divinely imposed duty of being an honest, noble and aspiring
man, strong in the principles and truths of a pure
manhood; I would see laws enacted and enforced to

do away with the heinous crimes of money speculations, and the riches of the land properly distributed, and for this reason do I lend my feeble voice and pen in humanity's cause. Mankind have been long enough slaves to a false system of living; the code social has imposed its restraints, set its bounds, and retarded man's progress to a very great extent ; but now that he is getting to be a *reasonable* and highly intellectual being, he must assume the rights vouchsafed to him in his creation, and stand forth a *free man*, nor longer be a slave to *public* opinion, a slave to *worldly pride*, a slave to *wealth*, a slave to the *passions* and low animal propensities. He should aspire to something more noble, pure, and elevated.

Man must open his understanding to the *principles* of life, and their right application in matters of living, if he would emancipate himself from the many ills and wrongs that now burden and oppress him. The way is clearly open, the *good* is before him, if he can but assume *moral courage* enough to make the attempt, but whether he make it or not, his life ever stands before him, from which he cannot flee, and the deep-toned silence of the past stands sentinel over all his acts, ready to unbury them of the accumulated rubbish and filth of *time*, when he shall have shaken off the mortal coil, and hand them all over to him in eternity. What he *does*, and what he *is*, that will he see, and so will he be, when he passes into that *clime* where he will be constantly under the surveillance of a power more mighty than man, and whose commands he cannot evade.

CHAPTER IV.

RELIGIOUS SLAVERY.

I come now to the consideration of a most important topic, religion ; one which is vital to the interests of all, inasmuch as it concerns the *eternal* as well as temporal welfare of mankind ; is most nearly allied to the principles of human existence, and teaches the best manner of *temporal* living to the end that the immortal may be best attained. It is not only the most vital, but the deepest rooted among human institutions, exerting a power which moulds and makes, to a very great extent, the social elements of the civilized world ; therefore is it one which needs our most careful and candid investigation. Time *here*, we are told, is but the probationary existence of man, and popular religion *professes* to teach the best manner of *using* that time to the attainment of an *eternal* and bright inheritance in celestial abodes. How well it does so I purpose to investigate.

Before proceeding farther it is necessary to define the term *true religion*, that my readers may get some definite idea of the subject under consideration. I do not propose, however, to go into any learned dissertations of past history and far-fetched quotations, or, in other words, shall not resort to the mythologies and vague notions of the past to prove any thing, preferring to deal with *living* matter and principles, and scientific analysis, and through *philosophic* research set forth my position and define my terms. What ignorant bygone ages have thought respecting religion is no evidence to us of the nineteenth century; *our* investigations must be by *our own* perceptions, because the law and order of creation is progress, as most emphatically written with the finger of time upon all things, and therefore what *has been* is no proof whatever of what *is* or *will* be. The past had of knowledge and wisdom sufficient for *its* development, and it is as absurd to think that the enlightenment of the people of long gone ages is any guide for *us* to follow, as it would be to say there has been no progress. Either there *has* been progress made or there *has not*, and consequently the natural order of creation *is progression* or it is *not*. And who that has ordinary intellect and good sense can doubt for a moment which it is, for all can see and know that the affairs of life about them are ever changing, and new and improved things are constantly occurring in their midst, speaking an argument in favor of progression stronger than all the theories ever spun.

In my former chapters I have dwelt somewhat upon the laws of life as the *principles* of a *divine order* and *intelligence*, overruling and *inruling* all the creations of the world, to which man constitutes no exception. The same laws that hold good in respect to a world and the various ingredients therein, hold good also to him, for *he is* one of the ingredients of matter *physically*, and of *spirit* mentally, or immortally; therefore is the school from which he must draw his truthful lessons of life wrapped up within the nature *from* whence he came, and *to* which he belongs.

The immortal principles of life from which he had being, compose the spiritual power, the intelligence, that compiles the body and resides therein for a time, and then takes its immortal flight to realms eternal, not far beyond the shores of time, but lingering upon its boundaries, still not removed from its precincts, for the dividing line between *time* and *eternity* is not capable of definition, save as seen in the separation of the spirit from the body,—the immortal from the mortal. *Time* and *eternity* continually join hands, and the step from the finite to the infinite but *one*. From this state of existence to the next, who shall calculate the distance or give bounds to the infinite? Does not earth swim in the ether blue, imbibing its spiritual life and light therefrom? Are not the God-given *principles of life* as much present *here* as in worlds unknown? Who is God, and whence comes 'life? Resides there an infinite Godhead in the unknown somewhere, from whose inexhaustible fountain are supplied all worlds with life? And who shall tell where is that fountain, that residence of life, love, and wisdom eternal? Certainly *not man*, for the little *world* in which he lives is beyond his full comprehension. And shall he fathom Deity? Oh, foolish and arrogant man! to presume to delve to Deific centres and bring to light the hidden mysteries of the eternal; to print, reprint, translate, time and again, the *edict* of an *infinite intelligence* to a *world's* people, while yet thine *own* centre of being is not explored, and the deep hidden life-powers of your own existence remain undeveloped! Foolish art thou, oh, man! in your ignorance, who would not presume to penetrate the divine cause of life, *if* but the knowledge of *little self* were more complete, for *then* would thy increased wisdom teach thee better. Man must deal with the known or surrounding elements of life before he can fathom to any extent the unknown. The *science* of *his own* existence must first be learned, and the revelations of an ever-revealing intelligent life-force in nature be his instructor. He lives in a growing, changing world, and the progress of time unravels the beautiful order and science of divine control to his enlarging perceptions continually.

Life is *internal*, life is spiritual, and ever developing from within outward; is a principle of eternal origin and eternal endurance. The great fund that constitutes immensity—so far as man's feeble perceptions go—and from which all material things receive vitality, the immeasurable ether, through whose spiritual depths traverse, in infinite order and harmony, myriads of worlds, orbs, suns, and comets, is the God we fable; an invisible, omnipresent, all-wise, all-intelligent, life-giving something, without which nothing lives,—a dual *power* embodying all the attributes of creation, call it air, vapor, gas, material or *non*-material, as you please, it still remains the fountain of life, life itself, *temporal* and *eternal*. A mysterious, indefinable, *self-sustaining*, *self-adjusting* combination of life powers, where whose first, great, originating fountain-head is man

3*

knows not. So far does human language serve me in expressing *my* ideas of God, of life, love, light, knowledge, wisdom, and power, and the nearest to any thing definite in expression I can arrive at, is in conceiving *two powers*, a *positive* and *negative*, keeping ever an *equilibrium* in their blendings, which seems very reasonable, since we cannot deal with and comprehend *matter* without discovering there to be always *two* conditions, *magnetic* and electric, or, in *animate* existence, male and female; and thus we can conceive of nothing which has not *two* extremes, *two* sides, ends, *two conditions;* therefore shall I call the Deific Power magnetism and electricity; magnetism being the *positive* and electricity the negative, one heat, the other cold; one, one extreme, and the other, the opposite extreme, in whose beautiful *mean* of *blending* is possessed all the attributes of the *universe.*

I do not mean to be understood to say, that there are two distinct elements of life, standing alone, or separate, for such is not the case; the forces of life, of nature, of God are ever blended and blending, so that what is positive to one condition is negative to another, and *vice versa;* and thus there is an eternal or infinite condition of developments, nothing being so positive that it is not negative still to a greater, and nothing so negative that it does not remain positive still to something lesser, and so is the chain of life complete—all conditions blended, all blending constantly, changing, obeying the reciprocal laws, and forming the great, eternal circle of creation.

Seemingly, man is dust and to dust returns, but

spiritually the spark that lights up his soul and lends
to the *inner* man *immortality*, is a *spiritual atom*
from the infinitude of space, in the ethereal depths of
which is his infinite home, where, as a spirit identity,
embodying intelligence, he resides, subject to the
ever increasing growth and progressive changes inci-
dent to the Eternal.

Man's life, then, is *in rapport* with the divine, subject to divine laws, which work *in, through,* and over
him continually, to expand, grow, and complete his
development constantly *towards* the infinite. Life
with him is a principle, a spark from the great fount
of the immortal, to *ever remain* among the never-
dying *vital* elements, and *not* a myth, a bauble to be
looked at superficially, *educated* superficially, and
superficially adorned for a few fleeting years, and at
last be blown away into annihilation by the autumn
winds of a short, superstitious, superficial existence.
No! Man always existed as a *principle* in the elements of creation, and his birth into earth-life but the
identifying of that principle into the *individual*, and
passing through a season of growth and individualized
refinement, preparatory to the borning again into
spirit reality. He is ever possessed of *immortality*
and the journey through earth-life but the shaping
into *identified* development, possessed of an intelligence nearest allied unto the infinite. He is not of
miraculous birth any more than all creation, but, in
the natural order of divine control, comes as the
climax of creative wisdom, in whom is embodied the
highest intelligence of *individualized Deific life*

power. Man is a microscopic atom compared with immensity, and yet a cosmos, combining in his organism all the principles of life beneath him, because standing at the *summit* of progressive order, the *result* of all the evolutions and changes of the life powers prior to him.

Seeing man in his true light and relations to the world of life about him, is to see his true character, position, and destiny : therefore the understanding of his *right culture* is easy. We see that to live in accordance with the divine principles of his being is clearly his duty to himself and his God, that he may fulfil well the object of his creation, and thus arise to the acme of human wisdom, a highly intelligent, honest, moral, and *religious* being. He springs from the divine fountain, and *to* the divine power *only*, through the laws of his being does he owe allegiance, *giving which* he fulfils the *reciprocal relations* between himself and his fellow-men ; therefore do I define *true religion* to be *true living*, and *honest work true worship*.

Action is the watchword of life, and humility, charity and love its attendants. *True* knowledge is real wisdom, and that knowledge only is true which teaches the *science* of *life*, and consequently true living. The *spiritual* lies ever back of, or within the physical, and is the motive power to action that evolves from chaos—undeveloped—order, harmony, and life progressive ; consequently the study of *spiritual* science gives that knowledge and wisdom to man which is eternal. It is this study that con-

stitutes *true religious teaching*, and applying which
to his practical concerns of life, gives to him the most
rapid unfoldment as an *enlightened and civilized*
human being. Such study gives the best and highest
culture to man, for it teaches him truly of the *life
within*, of the immortal, and raises him from the low
animal feelings and selfish tendencies of half developed animal man, because it *spiritualizes* him, and
creates aspirations which elevate him to the plane of
advanced, refined manhood. Such study again, and
spiritual teaching—*spiritual* because teaching the
cause and effect of man's existence, and the true tendency of his advancement, unravelling the mysteries
of his own being—is effective in enlightening and re-
forming mankind, simply because a *natural* and easy
manner of *speaking truth*, and giving that light which
can never be hid "under a bushel," or confined to the
narrow limits of a creed or ceremony.

Truth is the Almighty's weapon with which he brings
to stern justice all things, and thinkest thou, oh, man!
that thou canst escape its penetrating search, and go
unpunished for your errors and deceits? Thinkest
thou the self-adjusting laws of a just God thou canst
evade? I tell thee no; for divine order and harmony
will not allow that any of the cogs in the multiform
wheels of time should long be misplaced or missing.
Every thing receives its proper adjustment sooner or
later, and man surely finds *his* proper level.

Life is change, and constant motion the order of the
universe; nothing can remain *still*, for the watchword of the Eternal is forward! The earth, nor any

of the universal bodies remain motionless for an instant; but ceaselessly, sublimely, and eternally do they jaunt their endless round, over whose mighty movements and grandest results, *silence*, deep-toned and supreme silence, stands sentinel.

Were one to stand still for a moment, even, as the sun is *said* to have done at the command of the man Joshua, there would instantly be disorder in the whole, and the perpetual motion of the universal bodies destroyed. There is *system, science, order,* and *harmony* with the infinite control, and the Deific life elements are *unceasingly* working out the great problem of creation, which is too extended for man's full comprehension, and yet too minute and ethereal for his *senses* to realize. The *physical* is tangible to his physical senses; the spiritual is comparatively unexplored and uninvestigated.

By the sciences of life we learn, that there are no fixtures in the infinite plans; that what relates to the *eternal* is *eternally* in *action*, therefore the spirit, or *intelligence* of man, being, as we have seen, a *spark* from the *infinite* fund, an *immortal atom* of *individualized Deific life principle*, must be ever on the progress, ever *active* in *living* and *obeying* the laws of its *nature;* consequently *any thing* that tends to its *unchanging routine* of *action*, tends also to interfere with and destroy for a time its onward march, and therefore its best spiritual advancement, which we see cannot be its *truest religious culture*, because religious discipline pertains to the control of the *physical*, *through* the *spiritual* understanding and enlightenment, which spiritual order we have seen to be ever *active, progressive,* and unfolding. Set or fixed dogmas and routines do not accomplish this, therefore are they not only dead and false to what they profess, but *positively injurious* by interfering with *natural law* and growth.

Profession is one of the deceits and falsities of *man* and does not exist among *eternal principles.* With the divine, *every thing* is ACTION, and with nothing save man is there profession ; professing often to do what he does not, at least so in the matter of *popular* religion, which *professes* to teach the *spiritual* truths of man's existence, while it does not do so, but rather benights his understanding and retards his growth. *Professions* pass for nothing, and are mere mockeries, absurdities, and blasphemies when applied to *religion,* because the higher divine laws of our lives do not exact *profession,* but ACTION, *right action.* It matters not what we *profess,* so long as the *action* is *right* and *just,* is in accordance with the demands of our nature. Man's spirit *is* either immortal or it is not ; *if* immortal, it must be and *is* subject to the laws of *immortality,* therefore it cannot be rightly *cultivated* while *regulated* by ideas that are *fixed,* by *forms* that belong to superficial things, and *made by man,* without regard to or knowledge of the infinite laws, but pertain wholly to *worldly* aggrandizement and power, which aggrandizement and power promulgate avaricious and selfish feelings, and therefore *debase* the *spiritual.*

To study the higher, *spiritual,* inner laws of being, to know self thereby, and act in accordance therewith, is the *right* culture and understanding of ourselves. Whether the institutions of popular religion do this, I shall endeavor to determine.

If the physical is temporal, and the spiritual eternal, containing the life and power *of* the physical, it certainly is most desirable and dutiful to cultivate the *physical* in accordance with the laws of the *spiritual*, a good spiritual understanding being endurable riches, because giving that which nothing else can give— growth in *divine* order and fulness.

Worldly things, weighed by spiritual balance, are only worth what they serve in *forwarding* the *spiritual advancement*, nothing more; for the worldly ever changes, passing from form to form of different value constantly in the eternally changing order of things, so that the spirit of man cannot possess the interest of the world *as material*, and *only* as the circumstances of *time*, surrounding his physical condition, aid on the growth of the spiritual. Physical things administer to man's material needs, and justly so, but the spiritual endureth forever, while the physical is soon lost to him, therefore is it most highly important for him to rightly cultivate and understand the *spiritual;* so that, when he properly uses the physical, that is, with a good understanding of the spiritual, he really and truly *lives*.

True religion, then, teaches simply *true living*, and the homage and worship we are to render in life is right *action*, not *meaningless profession;* that *action* which controls the *physical* in harmony with the *spiritual*. True religion is to worship " in *spirit* and in *truth*," that is, to accord all our *physical* actions with *spiritual truths*. *Spirit* is *life, light, love, knowledge, wisdom,* and *power,* understanding which places us in harmony, or at-one-ment with the vast spirit of Deity.

There is no virtue in *profession,* for that power that·evolves all the universal creation, order, harmony, beauty, and sublimity, is *action,* constant and progressive *action*. The world of life in which *we* live is constant toil; *action* marks every phenomenon, from its own rotary motion down to the meanest growth within its nature. The seasons come in regular and beautiful succession, bringing their mighty changes; summer fills the land with the beautiful and useful, which stern winter, with its frosts and damps, decomposes to fertilize the earth for a new successive growth of a still higher development, and thus *time* marks its *eternal* course with seasons of *action, action,* never-ceasing *action,* growing and decomposing without cessation. Ah! how sublimely beautiful is the contemplation of nature, in her majestic and scientific order of *action!* We witness in her no professions, but in deep silence does she evolve all her varied changes. *Silence,* here, too, stands sentinel over all the mighty efforts, which bring forth from the womb of nature the sublime, the beautiful, and the useful. Grand and highly instructive lessons does nature continually unfold for man's study and enlightenment. The fount of all knowledge and wisdom is in her boundless recesses, and in her great laboratory is every possible unfoldment of science being wrought out to view, when man's comprehension shall be able to receive her teachings. Man receives every thing through his reason, can get nothing in any other way; the great chart of nature lies spread out continually before him, he lives upon it, it is the book for him to read, therefore let him reason and investigate; every hour spent in divining her secrets is better than gold to him, because learning that which gold cannot purchase.

The *morality* of a people is just in proportion to their *spiritual* enlightenment. The *study* of *self*, and of *nature*, learning the laws that govern, gives this spiritual knowledge, for in the phenomena of nature do we witness the operations of Deific power—God speaking to us in every act of the natural world. The *action* of Almighty control is ever visible, making the life, shaping and refining the world.

There needs no farther proof that the order of life is *action*, and *not profession*, therefore all the religious teaching in the world, having for its object the *practice* of meaningless professional *routine*, the constant *repetition* of senseless forms and ceremonies, is false to the cause, the furtherance of which it professes to exist for, viz.: SPIRITUAL *advancement;* consequently every thing connected with church, which is founded upon written records of the PAST, tied to the UNCHANGING dogmas of a defunct age, *without growth, without life, without progress, without philosophy, science, reason,* and *action,* when held up in the light *of* reason, philosophy, and *spiritual truth,* is, upon its face, *worldly* and *unmistakably worldly* in its *tendency,* because keeping its devotees in *igno-*

rance of the very *truths* which it *professes* to teach. Edifices of *costly* structure are set apart for *professional* worship, within whose sacred (?) precincts the draperies of the artist, and magnificent ornaments of the architect all speak of *worldly* riches, pride and pomp, and upon their highly cushioned seats, their folds within, recline the rich world's people with placid ease; while, perhaps, just outside the doors of those costly stone houses of God (?), filled with men and women ornamented with a suffusion of rich and fashionable dress, are *poor people*, actually hungering for bread! Oh! looks this like the Christianity Christ taught us? like the humility, benevolence, and charity of the lowly Nazarene? Methinks not; but on the contrary, how different from his example; how different from the great temple of nature, whose architect and artist is God, where all may live and worship truly according to the *divine* impulse of their natures, "without money and without price." Here are no front seats, reserved for the highest bidder in dollars and cents; no robed priestly *man* to din superstitious scares, raked up from the mythologic lore of the dark ages, of an awe-striking character, for a little worldly power; no *imaginative* hell-painted chasms, yawning their frightful abysses beneath your feet, but the free winds of heaven administer the cooling and refreshing draught of life and health, the singing birds sing sweet songs of freedom and love, the majestic hills, waving trees, and babbling brooks in glen and vale, tell of a power more grand and sublime than that of puny man, and a religion more true, more elevating and lasting than the wily impositions from sacred desks. There is no slavery, rank, and fashion in *true religion;* it exacts no professions, no dollars, no routine duties of forms and *man-made* creeds, but leaves the mind free to penetrate to the inmost depths of its own nature, and bring forth the hidden mysteries of being; to fathom and understand the laws of that being by means of its own *in*herent faculties of *reason* and intellect, and follow out the native impulse of a *growing* spirit, true to the laws of its own life.

God dwells in no temple apart, but is contained in the immensity of creation—as much here as there; not cloistered within church walls, not approached by *certain forms* and *rituals*, and not a *respecter* of *persons*, but is with each and every one in the laws of their existence, demanding of them nothing but exact obedience to those laws.

True religion is a thing that cannot be set apart from the common interest and best welfare of mankind, for it is a *spiritual knowledge*, which pertains to and concerns one as well as another, is inseparable from the duties and destinies of all, a thing of divine inheritance, which no man can take away; *not* gained through any beliefs in a vicarious atonement, or the infallibility of a *written*, dead word, but *indwells* in the human soul, a part of life, life its very self, to be *lived out* in *just action*, and with a *right* understanding. How different are the prevailing methods of *obtaining* so-called, religion—making *theories*, and *fencing them in!* Spirit, intangible and immortal, doled out by a few priests from the sacred (!) desk to

the masses, consisting in fine shows, forms, ceremonies, and *routine*, tread-mill *professional* duties, *im
posed* only *by man !*

As we have seen in a previous part of the writing,
that there are ever two powers ruling the creation—a
positive and negative; so there are two great parties
ruling the moral world, God and the priests; but as I
believe *God* to be the positive, supreme power, I shall
take sides with Him, thinking that, as He made the
world, and *also* the *priests,* He best knows how to
govern it.

The clergy are *men* of the *world*, as much as other
men, dipping in its scheming affairs quite as much—
bargaining, selling, and massing money often by speculations—travelling with, and being as those of the
world whom they profess to teach *spiritual* enlightenment—men among men in all the *mad civilization*
of the times, and then, once or twice in seven days,
aspire hypocritically to teach *spiritual* science and
truths ! " *Man cannot serve God and mammon !*"
If he is like the world, as it goes, he is *not* the spiritual philosopher he *should* be to truly teach spiritual
truths ; and if he *is* the spiritual philosopher, he cannot
honestly and conscientiously be like the world, partici-
pating in all its erroneous customs and follies ; therefore I have the right to say a man is hypocritical who
practises the one and *professes* the other, for they are
in very many things at least, diametrically opposed.
A man cannot be true to the *higher principles* and
laws of his nature, and at the same time be like many
of the prevailing customs of the age, for no one who

wishes to see, can but know, that the systems of living, of business, of education and religion, are sadly deficient. *Money* is the grand object sought, and its acquirement a matter of *surety* rather than *honesty*, too often.

Man cannot be truly spiritual, that is, true to the divine laws of his being, and at the same time be going the way of the world, and be any thing but a hypocrite, for then his *actions* belie his better spiritual understanding.

Our systems of education are sadly deficient ; instead of teaching *living* truth, *living* philosophy, educating the reason and intellect, they are founded *fundamentally* upon popular religion, and upon the verbatim acquirement of *written* school-book knowledge, which never had, so far as its *spiritual* understanding or teaching is concerned any just origin. The conceptions of school-book writers are generally those of church bigots, seeing every thing through the contracted avenues of their own minds, made so by *their* early training.

In the first place, almost all so-called educated men are taught religious dogmas from the time they are old enough to repeat the "Lord's Prayer" until arriving at mature years, and those religious ideas are simply certain faiths in an old traditional record—I say traditional because ancient history proves it *exclusively* so—called the Bible, for the truth and authority of which there never has been any *reasons* given, save the saying of the priests, that *it is God's word*, and at *their* say-so must be believed, and

their forms and ceremonies, based thereupon, be ad-
hered unto, or *else* humanity must be damned!

These ideas concerning Deity and his instructions,
and *their* worship, are assiduously and *in*sidiously
inculcated into the young mind until they become a
second nature,- that is, supplant the *natural aspirations* and give bias to the mind for a lifetime. Human nature is *naturally* religious, and the inherent
sentiments of reverence in the young are easily
wrought upon and moulded, doing which has been
the object and work of the ministry for centuries.
Upon these popularly and thoughtlessly accepted doctrines of religion the various systems of education are
founded, giving no chance to the natural, inherent tendencies,—which are ever good if only left *free* and
taught *truth*—to aspire in the direction of the *really*
spiritual, so that the young are moulded and their
minds stultified by teaching them a *dead letter*, a
dead religion, which arrive at no real spiritual facts
by dint of philosophic investigation and inquiry, but
simply say *believe*, have *faith* and *reason not*, and you
shall be saved! Believe in what? I would ask. Why
that what the ministers tell us concerning an old
compilation from the dust of ages, called Bible, is
living truth, is the word and instructions of an infinite God to a finite people, all enclosed in a small
volume which a person can carry in the pocket—a
pigmy representation of divine revelation when compared to the great and LIVING chart of nature—a
guide for all time to come, for a *progressive people*,
and ask no questions of a *philosophic* nature. Popu-

lar religion does not admit of scientific questioning, as the investigations of geology, astronomy, and all the sciences prove, for science is simply the unravelling of Nature and learning her truths, which at the same time unravels popular Christianity and reveals its fallacies, showing it to be a *man-made* institution, having for its object worldly power, and *not* spiritual advancement, and in no way connected with the beautiful laws and truths of Deity; bears in it nothing of science or spiritual philosophy. No, indeed! it would be like nursing the adder at the breast to put science among religions, for their life-currents would be so poisoned from the stings of the *adder* of *truth*, that soon would they go into convulsions which would end their rotten existence.

I am asked, perhaps, what I would substitute in place of the present prevailing systems of religion, as a restraint to wrong tendencies. What substitute? good heavens! what could be substituted *justly* but *truth*, beginning with the young mind, and teaching it the truths of its own existence; giving it spiritual insight into the laws of its own being. What do? teach *truth* instead of *falsehood*, instead of superstition, and forms, routines, and tread-mill duties, and soon would be apparent the progress of mankind in right directions; soon would the moral worth of humanity be very much improved, and the races of men and women become noble specimens of elevated, refined, and spiritualized human beings. But cease teaching the young dogmas which place them in false relations to their own natures, and give them instead, inculcations of *God's* universal truths, and see how soon they will grow to be humane, charitable and real Christ-like beings.

If the young were rightly educated, by teaching them first the simple truths of their own organisms, and to deal with the world of life about them upon just principles *inherent* in the human soul, there would be no necessity for the temperance lecturers and various local reformers that now traverse the land, trying to do away with the *effects* of a wrong system of education, while the *causes* are still in force. Until *causes* are removed, *effects* will continue. If children are taught wrong ideas from infancy concerning life and a Deity, and to revere those wrong ideas as an indefinable awe, a spell put upon them by the clergy, of course, they are warped out of their natural inclination of mental vigor, and a bias given which is very apt to follow them through life, unless it is now and then a mind possessed of great native strength of intellect, which all the long-instilled dogmas of old theology failed to crush out.

The slavery imposed by popular religion thus begins in early childhood, and is so thoroughly inculcated as to supplant the *natural aspirations*, and in adult age is borne through sheer ignorance of the higher, nobler, better *religion* of *nature*. It becomes a time-worn custom with them, and is followed from force of *habit* rather than *reason:* indeed, reason would soon clash with its falsities and find out its absurdities. But *reason*, that God-like faculty of the human soul, is very seldom used to any extent, be-

4

cause early crushed out by the instillation of. superstitions and forms, of routine duties, imposed by the
ministry, and enforced by parents.

We study into the science of life, and bring to light
the truths of nature and then we see every thing *free*,
acting according to the wise laws of a creative wisdom; in all the kingdoms of nature is life free save with
mankind : here a few hold sway over the many, keeping them in mental servitude by means of long imposed superstitions and doctrines concerning a *personal*
God, who, they tell us, is pleased or *wrathful*, according as we follow out the meaningless *ceremonies* of
church or *not*.   Ceremonies and customs by which the
few keep up *their* worldly power and support.

Let us look into this matter of *routine, professional*
religion a little more closely, and see how well it cor-
responds with good sense, philosophy and reason.
And I commence with the assertion, that God made
and now governs the world by laws which work in
order, harmony, and beauty ; therefore if he intended
mankind should have any *set form* of worship, any
more than living out the laws of their natural lives,
why has He not given that form in a *definite* and distinct instruction, so that all may know the *proper*
manner of doing the reverence he demands ?   Does
the creative wisdom-principle work by order, exactness, and decision, or is creation left at loose ends, with
nothing definite ?   If by order and decision—which
every phenomenon of nature proves—then why in the
matter of religion, that of all other concerns it is
most essential we should *rightly* know, has Deity left

us to gain a *form* as we may? In other words, if He *is* all order, conciseness, and decision in every thing else, why not so in religion? Is religion, or *right living*, of so little moment that it is unnecessary to have any divine instructions given concerning it? Perhaps it will be said, that we have ample instructions in the Bible, which are concise and plain; then if so, I would ask why so many *different* forms and creeds in the world?—about six hundred—for if God *has* given any instructions for a *particular form* of worship, then *one* only of all the prevailing creeds— that is, if His is known—must be *right*, and all the others necessarily *wrong*, so that only about one-sixth part of all the *professed* Christians are really so; now, which of the six hundred is *right*, or established by God, is the question—a question which has been much discussed by the clerical profession, and which *all* claim to have settled in their *own* favor, therefore it is proper to infer that *all* are wrong, and that *none* are strictly founded upon the great *progressive* and harmonious laws of *nature*. These are important questions, if there is any truth in the prevailing theology, but if it is as rotten as it appears to be, then it is not worth questioning.

If, on the contrary, there is no God-given creed— save the observance of the laws of our nature—which every scientific investigation proves, and every phenomenon of life distinctly avows, then what must be the terrible sins to answer for, by those whose whole lives are spent in the study and investigation of this very matter of religion, and who *should* know, and *do* know what they teach, and still persist in building MAN-*made creeds*, and from the so-called, sacred desk from Sunday to Sunday, imposing them upon the ignorant world's people *as God's requirements* of them! They tell you that to be saved, and thus avoid that horrible hell they *picture*, in which all who are not *Christians* are *eternally* damned, you must enter the *church*, take oaths of allegiance, and pay your *dollars* for *its* support, which is simply the support of a set of professional *men*, too lazy to get their living in any honorable way—by *real* and WORTHY *toil*.

Oh! what a curse to humanity is that teaching, which blights and benights the *spiritual* understanding, and makes *bigots* of God's free and noble souls. Either there *is* a *God-given* creed of *particular* forms and rituals, or there *is not*. Now, ye priestly throng! take which horn of the dilemma you choose. If there *is*, then the whole civilized world must know it, as it is given *to* the world for man's guide, and of *itself* would be the *civilizing* and *enlightening* power *of* the world, *consequently* there could be no *variance* of creeds, forms, and ceremonies, but all people would come under *one* creed, and *that* the *Divine*; therefore there is no God-given creed of *particular* form, as the evidence of the worldly creeds prove by their *numbers* and *distinctions*. On the contrary, if there is no divine creed of set forms, then what blasphemers and mockers are ye, to impose *your own* senseless forms, under the garb of *divine* religion, in the stead of Deity's beautiful laws of nature, and wise instructions, which gleam forth in every phenomenon of universal power and life. These are grave considerations, and should command the most careful investigation of all men and women, for it is a matter of much importance to us all, whether we shall be longer held in mental slavery, and the best spiritual aspirations of our natures crushed out by false teachings, or whether the *mind* shall be left *free*, and given that expansion and scope for thought, that enables it to delve into and understand the laws of its own condition.

It is time the shackles of old theology were shaken off the mind, and the restraints and false teachings it imposes done away with, which, thank higher power, is fast approaching.

Why! look abroad upon the world and witness the grandeur, beauty and sublimity of creation; ask philosophic questions concerning the cause of all this, measure with the science of astronomy feebly, the vast distances of the orbs and worlds of the universe from each other; contemplate the supreme power that keeps such a stupendous machinery in motion where the different parts are millions and billions of miles apart, and yet the order and harmony, the never-ceasing *action* is perfect; I say, contemplate this magnificence of the creation by first viewing the dimensions of our own small earth, and then comparing it, as a *part*, to the *whole ;* let the mind stretch into unfathomable abyss and imagine the glory and majesty of the *supreme power*, that has neither beginning nor end, who is all life, all love, all goodness, all harmony, all order, exactness, conciseness and science, and then turn the thoughts within little *self*, and by means of the sciences of anatomy and physiology, note its wonderful mechanism: reflect that *its* science of life is a part of the illimitable science and mystery of the infinite, and after dwelling until the mind is in awe and wonder at the power, vastness, and beauty of universal life, then narrow it down to a church creed, contemplate in turn the routine, sesame performances of *its* order, and draw conclusion between *its* narrow ideas, its limited notions of God, heaven— an eternal city *paved* with *gold!* hell, a vicarious atonement, infant damnation, a wrathful, *personal* Deity, who, dressed in the garb of orthodoxy, possesses more *changeableness*, fickleness, and unmerciful atrocities than Satan himself; exacting a rigid, senseless *church* obeyance, or else sending his children to an eternal hell of torment! I say to my readers, contemplate all the foregoing, and then ask yourselves how well the present popular Christian teachings compare with the sublimity, beauty, science and wondrous order and action of *creation*.

A little common sense is the antidote to much evil, and applied to religion shows up its inconsistencies, absurdities, fallacies, and falsities, and scatters its power to the four winds of heaven, as the morning sun dissipates the dew-drop.

All this *church* religion is founded upon a book, which existed in the ancient fables and traditions, to a very great extent, thousands of years before the *Christian* era; a book containing accounts of murders, robberies, wars, obscenities; of inconsistencies, lies, contradictions, and vulgarities, which no other book equals,

and yet it is revered as the word of God—a *personal*
God. All *science* proves my *assertion*, history its
certainty, and were other and surer proof needed, it
is only necessary to look at *its own internal evidence*,
which is discoverable by reading carefully and criti-
cally, to any one who has ordinary common sense and
reason. I know I shall be harshly criticised for
speaking so *irreverently* of the Bible, notwithstanding
it is the *truth*, which every person who has *really
read* the Bible could testify to ; those who have never
read it of course know nothing concerning it, save
what they *believe*, and therefore their opinions are
worth nothing. So far as the Bible contains *truth*, I
revere it, as I would the *truth* under any circumstances, but because there *is* truth sprinkled through it,
am I obliged to believe all its falsehoods? What
mother or father would wish their daughters or sons
to read the Bible from the beginning to its end, and
practice every thing they read? Because there is
some good precepts contained in it which are worthy
of imitation, would they wish their children to imitate
and follow *all* its instructions? *If* they *are* the instructions of Deity, should they not all be followed?
Or shall man *dictate* to *Deity* by choosing what por-
tions of its instructions he will follow? I will here
give one extract from the *Bible* concerning the return
of the Jewish army from one of its murdering and
plundering expeditions, found in Numbers, chap.
xxxi., ver. 13–18.

" And Moses, and Eleazer the *priest*, and all the
princes of the congregation, went forth to meet them

without the camp; and Moses was wroth with the officers of the host, with the captains over thousands, and captains over hundreds, which came from the battle; and Moses said unto them, *have ye saved all the women alive ?*   Behold, these caused the children of Israel through the counsel of Balaam, to commit trespass against the Lord in the matter of Peor, and there was a plague among the congregation of the Lord; now therefore *kill every male among the little ones, and kill every woman that hath known man by lying with him; but all the women-children, that have not known a man by lying with him, keep alive for yourselves.*"

Among all the horrible scenes that ever disgraced the records of history, I think it would be impossible to find a more damnable and disgraceful one than that here recorded of Moses.   Let any mother imagine herself in the situation of those mothers; one child murdered outright, another destined to brutal violation, and herself in the hands of the executioner; let any daughter place herself in the situation of those daughters, a prey to the infamous and hellish purposes of the *murderers* of her *mother* and brother, and what would be their feelings?   Could they feel that the enormous outrages committed were in accordance with the commands of a just God, a God of *love* and *mercy*, a moral and humane God?   It is worse than folly to impose thus upon human nature, for it has a sanctity of feeling, an inherent moral and religious sentiment, that revolts at the mere *recital* of such heinous and barbarous tortures; and thus I *might* go on making similar extracts from the Bible enough to fill my volume; and because I here *quote* them *verbatim*, rehash them to the enlightened ear and eye of the nineteenth century, is it sacrilege? is it awful? cannot I read *my* Bible and have my *reason* in it, my mind concerning it, without the fear of *man* before my eyes? Ay! *Truth* is stronger than all beside. I write for the good of my brother man, for his elevation, and because I do thus it is that I would have him understand his *nature*, and not longer have it imposed upon by such infamous stuff as I here quote, under the long-instilled belief that it is the *word* of *God*. I would see every man exercising his *own* mind, using his *God-given* faculties and not allow any of his rights to be usurped by others of his own kind and race no better than himself.

According to the 35th verse of the same chapter, the number of women-children consigned to debauchery by the order of Moses was *thirty* and *two thousand*. All this is the work of Moses, who is the paragon of excellence of character and *inspiration* among the famous men of the Old Testament; a man who, the *Bible says*, talked face to face with God!

It is astonishing how gullible are human beings upon this topic of Bible and religion, while constantly using reason and good sense in every other concern of life. Yet I see why it is so: the insidious inculcations of wily *men*, moral scavengers, into the young mind from childhood up, makes *thinking* upon this one thing out of the habits of living, and consequently people in general know not what wickedness there is in this *pretended* word of God. Brought up

4*

in habits of superstition, they take it for granted that
the Bible is true, and carry the ideas they form of the
goodness and charity of the Almighty to the book,
which they are taught to believe was written by His
authority. Good heavens! it is quite another thing;
it is a record of lies, barbarous atrocities, and blasphemy; for what can be greater blasphemy than to
ascribe the wickedness of *man* to the orders of the
"God of Love," as in the instance of Moses, which I
have quoted?

I speak strong language, for it is time strong words
were used, fearlessly used, and the impositions which
have been for so long a time, and still are being prac-
ticed upon my fellow-beings demand my utterance in
their behalf: I cannot idly sit and see the young
mind put into mental slavery in infancy almost,
which darkens and benights its growing understanding, by a set of men whose object it is to obtain
worldly power, and a living, for I see that it is unjust
and contrary to every divine teaching, contrary to
science and philosophy, good sense and reason, and
my soul cries out against the enormous evil. What
but for this mental slavery, this stultifying of the
spiritual faculties, might not humanity become? If
left free to mature their minds in the strict observance
of the laws of life, how fast would they shoot ahead
in knowledge and wisdom, and *true* civilization and en-
· lightenment take the places of bigotry and superstition.

Man is *naturally* kind, noble and pure, were it
not for the base intrigues of his *brother* man, cheat-
ing him of his hard-earned dollars, benighting his

spiritual understanding and keeping him grovelling in the dust, giving him tendencies to selfishness, licentiousness, and the commitment of *all* crimes, for that teaching which keeps the mental capacities in the dark; keeps down the culture of the spiritual faculties, gives rise to evils innumerable, because *not* giving real and true enlightenment and growth to the mind. In proportion as man understands the laws of his being, and his spiritual perceptions are enlarged to comprehend the true source of life and his relations thereto, just in that degree is he a good man, living honestly, and for the good of his brother man as well as his own; but that teaching which stints and contracts the mind by holding it in bondage to certain *worldly* ideas instead of PRINCIPLES, tends to make rogues and unprincipled men.

To rear *good* children it is only necessary to observe the laws of life in *marrying* and *procreating*, and then, when born, teach them the simple truth, teach them nature and the knowledge it reveals: teach them *principles* instead of creeds and dogmas, and by *reason* and *philosophy* educate the intellect. But this is now prohibited: old theology stands at the very foundation of all schools, and instills its poison into the young mind before it is old enough to reflect, and the consequence is, teachers are bigots mostly, and the systems of education matters of *form* quite as much as real learning. The mind is kept so constantly under the influence of religious teachings which are *contrary* to *nature* and *philosophy*, that it loses, to a very great extent, its power of reason and reflection, because losing its natural spiritual aspirations; it learns to view every thing as *material*, believing God to be more in the priest and church and unknown somewhere, than in the scientific studies it follows; therefore the life principle that quickens thought into acuteness is quenched out, and the mind left to grope among old, musty volumes and rigid *forms* of study, to the exclusion of all that beautiful and highly instructive *study* of *nature*, which lies all around in the world about, and is all *life*, knowledge, and wisdom.

As I glance back through the records of the past, I see that in every age of the historic world has the progress of civilization, and the diffusion of general knowledge been sturdily opposed by the clergy. No new discovery in science and literature, unless of an ecclesiastical nature, but what they have fought strenuously against, while every reformer and civilizer has shared their persecutions. The great Galileo, whose majestic mind peered into the vast and wonderful science of astronomy, and by means of the telescope, brought down the family of the heavens to the comprehension of man; Faust, whose art of *printing*, in the fifteenth century, was deemed and denounced by them as an invention of the devil; Newton, Mesmer, down to the eminent men of our own time, such as William Lloyd Garrison, Wendell Phillips, Theodore Parker, Ralph Waldo Emerson, and many others of eminence, have been alike subject to their abuses, bitter denunciations and uncharitable attacks, ill becoming the *professions* of those calling themselves priests of God.

and sitting in high places! Little, indeed, in any age of the world, have the clergy shown any thing like a *Christian* spirit, and *practised* what they *preach;* neither *now* do we find them any more liberal and charitable towards the advance of science, save that the popular intelligence will not allow them to say as much as formerly, yet they still use their influence in opposing every new thing in the scientific world, which does not accord with and uphold their *professions;* while the spirit of *real* Christian virtue is as little manifest as in olden times. They war not only with every progressive step in the outer world, but with each other, sect arrayed against sect, in most uncharitable terms.

Fortunately for the world, however, their opposition has proved inadequate to stay the rapid march of Science—the parent of all truth—the philosophic unfoldings of which is God's language to the world, and revelations to man. It has been the aim of the clerical profession not to advance science, but to oppose it and keep their adherents in bigotry as much as possible, for well they know, that in the ignorance of the people lies the secret of their power ; but *really* enlighten the popular mind in *true* spirituality—as I am most happy to know, is now being rapidly done —and the priestly power which now enslaves so many minds in spiritual *darkness*, will soon lose its influence so to do, and the common understanding be very much enhanced.

This religious slavery, I have said, is based upon a book *called God's word*, but really a book raked up and compiled from the fables and traditions of the dark ages, long before the Christian era began. Let us now look a little into the merits of the book, and see how well *it* bears out my assertion, for my statement is based upon historic lore. According to the account of *creation* given in the Bible the earth is only about six thousand years old, while really the length of time it has existed man cannot tell; but, by means of its own science, Geology, we know it to be *very much* older than the time here given, and the facts in relation to the history of the human race shows it to have existed thousands and thousands of years before the Bible account, at least four thousand years; while Geology discovers the fossil remains of man at least 35,000 years old, and, as has been stated by some investigators, 100,000 years. These are general hints at great and mighty facts, without going into detail, which the Bible can never overthrow, notwithstanding the antagonism of the two accounts, viz.: that which God has written, with the finger of time upon the long-buried and ever-living *tablets of nature*, and that written by ignorant *man* upon a *dead* page, a dying record, in a very stupid and blundering manner. Further, the absurdity of the Bible account is seen when it says, that in the beginning God created the heavens and the earth in *six days*, and the earth was *without* FORM and void,—imagine a thing without *form!*—and says the evening and the morning were the *first day*, and so on until the *fourth day*, when the sun was created. Now I would ask in all sincerity, how there could be morning and evening *without* a sun? and how the earth could have been made before the sun, when the science of Astronomy reveals to us the fact, that the sun is the *central* orb of this constellation, holding all the small orbs, among which is our earth, revolving in duty about it, and probably also being the *parent* of all the smaller orbs in its presence.

Again, I would ask in *what* beginning is meant, when it says, in the beginning, &c.? Further along it says Adam and Eve were the first human beings, and had two sons, Cain and Abel, but Cain killed Abel, leaving but three human beings *in the world*, for up to this time Seth, the *third* child, was not born; yet we are immediately told by the same record, that Cain, being driven from the Garden of Eden in consequence of having killed his brother, " went out from the presence of the Lord and dwelt in the land of *Nod*, on the *east* of Eden, and *knew* his *wife;*" which land of Nod was not probably far off, as they had no railroads in those days. Now in the name of truth, where did Cain get his wife IF Adam and Eve *were* the *first* human beings? He certainly did not marry his mother, for she remained in the Garden with Adam, while Cain " *went out*" from the Garden and found him a wife! All this, recollect, is *before* the birth of Seth, who was the *third* son, Gen. iv. chap., verse 25. And not until *after this* had Adam and Eve any daughters, chap. v., verse 4. And so from beginning to end, this *pretended* word of God, which has been imposed upon the people so long as such, is full of lies and inconsistencies, absurdities

and obscenities without parallel. It is nothing but
mere ignorance and superstition to believe such stuff
to be *God's* word ; for do you not suppose that God,
who is the mighty builder, controller, and sustainer of
the world, with its science, beauty, and perfectness,
could write a more consistent record than the Bible?
Ay! God does not write *words* for man save those
written in the phenomena, wonderful, beautiful, and
sublime, of universal law.   In the *science* of *creation*
may man ever read useful and truthful lessons of life,
of morals and religion, to *do which* he need not become a slave to a mess of *church* forms and ceremonies, senseless in the extreme.

Notwithstanding the palpable and glaring contradictions and ignorant inconsistencies of the Bible, *men,*
calling themselves intelligent, make its *study* and *research* a *profession,* and palm it off upon the ignorant
world's people for God's instructions to them!   I say
ignorant, for people are certainly ignorant concerning
the Bible, or they would not thus be deceived and imposed upon.   Can men, making this book a *life* study
be *honest* in representing it as God's word?   How
came the clergy to know more of God than other men,
that they can negotiate between earth and the Eternal?   Is Deity a *respecter* of persons, that he should
give to *them* only, that the rest might get it by hear-
say?   Ay! they even dictate to the Almighty, and
make Him do the most enormous crimes, such as
damning for all *eternity* the greater portion of his
children, *cursing* or *blessing* them according as they
follow after the *priests* or not, and go through *church*

forms: making also a portion of his children *elect;* others damned before they are born! They tell you that a man cannot enter heaven, or *happiness,* be he ever so good, unless he goes through church doors and prayers! in other words, unless he *pays* for it in *dollars* and *cents!*

How much, reader, does this look like your conception of a *just, supreme,* and good God, who is *all* LOVE! It smacks to my understanding over-much of worldly power and interest; of *aristocracy* and *man-government.* Man's *spiritual* understanding is his freedom; cramp *that* and he becomes a *mental slave.* Just in proportion as man learns the philosophy of his *own being* so does he become good, for he sees *laws* which he admires and loves, and aspires to be like. This, the prevailing theology does not teach: there is nothing of a philosophic nature in its instructions, but rather dead senseless *routine* and *form.* It dwells not upon *science,* nor teaches man any thing concerning his *nature,* present or future, but leaves him hanging on by means of *faith* and *belief,* to he knows not what! He is taught to have *faith* and be satisfied; and if his *faith* should fail to comprehend the whole *religious* system clearly, if his *reason* rebels and he becomes too *inquisitive,* excommunicate him from the order, as has been done in thousands of instances.

The moment a man in the church becomes any way LIBERAL in his views, begins to *think,* then is the church afraid of him, because it is dangerous to tolerate such *heresies* as *free thought* and *speech,* and if he will not

retract and succumb to priestly tyranny, then he must
be shuffled off, lest he contaminate others with his
God-given aspirations, free thoughts and liberal views.

Having glanced at the *beginning* of the Bible and
pointed to the *first* of its glaring inconsistencies and
untruthful statements, I come now to consider a few
of the ideas set forth in religious teachings. The human race, according to religious dogmas, dates from
the man Adam, whom the church advocates fabulously
place in the fabulous garden of Eden, and then fabulously state that from one of his ribs, extracted by
Deistic fingers, was made Eve, the first (fabulous)
woman, in whose sinning, through the beguilement of
the serpent, Adam was induced to partake of the
forbidden fruit—fabulous fruit also—and thus the
whole succeeding work of the Almighty, in making
human beings, became a failure from the beginning,
to partially reclaim which, he sent his son into *this
world* to DIE (!) that sinning mortals might be saved
in a fabulous heaven—in other words *immortality
died* for *mortality!* An improbable, *impossible,* and
fabulous story, concocted by the priests out of ancient
fables, as a *means* to gain power over the people. God
made the earth and all that is in it, including man and
woman, and "saw every thing he had made and behold
it was *very* good," all in *six* days—*our* days, because
they had morning and evening, sun and moon—and
notwithstanding "*it was very good,*" the *woman* he
had made outwitted him in the outset, and destroyed,
so far as human creation—which was the highest, and
therefore cost the greatest divine effort and labor—

was concerned, his sublimest effort, and not only so, but made it *necessary, imperatively* necessary—so that God is dictated to—for him to damn the greater portion of his creation of human beings for all time to come—or at least until popular Christianity shall have redeemed the world (!)—to eternal torment! What a sublime story!!! It is too foolish, ridiculous, and absurd to retain the candid belief of any *sensible* person for a moment. I should very much dislike to commit such blasphemy and sacrilege against *my* maker as to adhere to any suchworship or belief.

Let us now look a little into their wonderful doctrine of vicarious atonement, through which, *they* tell us, the world is to be reformed; at least some portion of it some thousands of years hence, perhaps; of course, the *past,* which has gone to its grave unshrived, is all *lost!*

Before Christ's birth into the world, there existed *two* Gods—so the story runs—who had an adversary in the form of the Devil, who was too much for them, that is, for God and Holy Ghost, and whose power of *destruction* was greater than these two gods to save, notwithstanding God was the Father of the Devil, as he is Father of *all* things, and therefore *another God* had to be created in the form of Christ, in order that the world might not be a total failure, wholly at the mercy of Mr. Devil! This is the *substance* of the priestly yarn, in brief. Now they tell us that these three Gods, Father, Son, and Holy Ghost, are *one!* formerly the Father and Holy Ghost were *one*, and *two*, but when a third was needed, then came Christ to make good the fable, and thus it runs : a virgin conceived and bore a son ; the father of this conception was Holy Ghost, that is, God conceived God (himself), with one of his *earth* children, Mary, and is therefore *his own author through the womb of a* MORTAL mother, for do they not tell us, these lucid priests, that there is but *one* God, and *still,* that God and the Son are one and the same, and equal ? Do they not tell us that there are a *trinity* of Gods and yet but *one?* Admitting the possibility of the conception, it looks like rather a shameful thing in Deity to *debauch* a *virgin,* and *she his own child;* think of it, Mary bearing her own father, God, and God his own conceiver, to say nothing of the *example* set. So that *now* we have three Gods, and still but *one,* that is, two and one added are *one,* and *one* by some inexplicable means is *three !* Now I think it would quite puzzle any scientific mathematician to reconcile this matter of orthodox Gods, by making one out of three, or three out of one.

Strange it is, that one *man* can tell another such palpable and absurd falsehood upon the face of it and be believed, because pointing to the Bible as authority, especially men calling themselves intelligent, and who *are really* so in other matters of life.

I have spoken of these things lightly, and yet as seriously as they will admit, for such stuff, called *religious teaching,* in the absence of all truth, admits of but one consideration at the hands of all candid people, and that is *ridicule;* it is open to nothing else, for it does not partake of *reason* or common sense.

How different such fabled nonsense, such unreason-
able stories, from the beautiful truths and philosophic
laws of nature! how narrow, superstitious, and bigoted! What does man know of himself when educated
through the church? how much of the philosophy of
life does he thus gain? How much *spiritual* understanding does he acquire? Oh! how much mental
darkness does he *not* acquire in relation to his spiritual
existence, by having his mind, from childhood up,
stuffed full of theologic lore (!) made up from such
absurd and ridiculous stuff as I have here shown.

I did not intend to touch so strenuously upon the
prevailing creeds at first, believing the best way to
reform is to bring in the *new*, and let *it* crowd out the
old, but after going somewhat into the philosophy of
true spiritual culture, and showing the laws of life in
their relations to human beings, it seemed necessary
that I should draw the comparison, and show how
widely apart and different in their teachings are the
two; one all *science*, *truth* and *natural*, the other all
ignorance, *superstition* and *artifice*. And, too, as I
am writing more for the emancipation of the mind
from bondage than the body, I cannot but dwell somewhat upon that custom and time-worn institution,
which most effectually enslaves the *mental*, and chains
down to egregious errors and lies, by means of long
practised cunning, man's noblest spiritual aspirations.
The physical slavery in our midst is nothing compared to the mental; is productive of not one-tenth part
of the wrong and mischief to humanity as mental
bondage; for the mental is superior to and controls

the physical, consequently, that teaching which benights the mind fits it to be a physical slaveholder. No man of *true* education could hold a slave, because a conscience which had been grown under proper culture would not tolerate the wrong, but with minds used to *mental* slavery, there appears no wrong in physical bondage; so that back of the palpable physical evils in the land is wrong spiritual education, or rather I should say, *professed* spiritual education, for that is *not spiritual* which teaches error, old fogyism, superstition, and non-progressiveism.

To emancipate the *mind* from the many wrong notions entertained respecting popular religion, is a much greater work than mere physical abolition, stupendous as that is; for errors inculcated into the young mind and followed until mature years become deep-rooted, and require much sturdy effort in their uprooting and clearing out, which forcible physical abolition will do much towards forwarding. A giant blow has been struck by the President of America—record it all ye angels of light—at the monster evil of physical servitude in the South, and the axe is being whetted which shall strike the death-blow at the root of the greater monster evil of mental slavery. The gateway of the understanding is being opened, and the darkness which has so long enthralled the mind, will be dispersed by the floods of spiritual light ushered in through philosophy and reason.

There is but *one* true religion, there can be but one, and that necessarily is that which is founded in the establishment of the world by the divine power, to know and follow which is true worship. *Religion* is not man made, but Divinity born, a moral attribute of the creation, and that set up by man without regard to natural law, what can it be but sacrilege and blasphemy? Either true religion is heaven born and belongs *naturally* with the human soul, or there is no religion, for if *God* has not established such a thing as worship, then *man's* inventions are *not* true religion, because not an *essential* part of our existence, not being instituted by God. I claim, however, that religion proper *is* a part of life, and the term rightly used means nothing more than *true living*, to do which is all the worship required of us by Deity, for that infinite power has placed us here *with laws* governing, and certainly laws would not have been given were they not for our obeyance; therefore what greater homage can we pay to the power supreme than the observance of those laws? Certainly nothing greater, and when *man*, in his selfish and wicked desires for power and gain, cunningly invents rituals and forms to impose upon his more ignorant brother man under the garb of religion, in the place of Deity's beautiful laws, what shall we call it? Is it *religion* or *not?* Is it *right* or *wrong?* Is it worship or blasphemy? And *does* it tend to open and enlighten the spiritual understanding or *not?* These are questions which every one should ask himself and herself, nor deem them answered until from the interior depths of their own souls, through *thought* and *reason*, the answer comes.

We are often told by priestly men, that we must not reason upon points of Scripture! what then must

we do, since man knows nothing except *by reason?*
Why, take *their* word for it! And pray how did
they arrive at the right or wrong of what they *profess* to teach? Was it by *faith* or reason? If by
faith, then reason at once rebels, and says it is not
worthy acceptance: if by reason, then again reason
says, I too, can reason: therefore, why are we told
not to reason? Manifestly to keep us in ignorance,
well knowing, as they do, that a little well directed
reason would soon explore and explode their frauds
and sham religions. Now, if man cannot *reason* upon
religious things, why upon other things? Why was
reason given him if not intended for use? and if for
use in *one* thing, why not in *all* things? If a man's
reason cannot tell him right and wrong, *what can?*
Is there any higher power in his possession than his
reason? Is not man the *highest* development of creation,—so far as *this* world is concerned—the acme of
all *embodied* intelligence, and is not *reason* the highest faculty of that intelligence, sitting in judgment
over all his other faculties? If so, then what shall
man know save he use his reason? We are also told
to have *faith* and believe. Believe what? is it possible to believe before we know, and can we know without the exercise of reason? No! We can have no
knowledge of even the slightest affair without the exercise of reason. If reason is to have no voice in religious affairs, and the Bible *is really* the inspired
Word of God, then it might just as well have been
given to the brutes as to man, for take away a man's
reason and what is he but a brute? Ay! a thorough-

ly insane man is worse than a brute, will commit
more brutal acts. Is it not reason that makes man
sane? and its deprivation *insane?* Thus the clergy
often attempt to exercise greater power over man,
greater tyranny, than a monarch, for they would deprive him, if possible, of his God-given *reason.*

Deprive our churches of their attraction save the
preached Gospel as it comes from ministerial lips, and
how many would attend them, how long would they
exist? Remove organ, architectural adornments,
fashion, dress parade, music, public opinion, and all
the incidental attractions, and leave nothing to draw
forth worshippers but the love of worship, and few indeed would attend, it would be so monotonous, sleepy,
and uninteresting! In short, popular religion without its adornments would become very soon unpopu-
lar. All this church show is nothing but an *aristocracy;* take away its aristocratic elements and it
would possess no power. Music is harmony of sounds
in keeping with nature's complete harmony, and is
worship, the only element of true religion in the
churches.

Science, philosophy, and nature are the guides to
true living, and therefore to *true religion* and *civilization.* It is very easy to *profess* religion, putting
on its *popular appearance one* day in seven, and, perhaps, be a rascal the other six, but to be the *true*
Christian, that is: *Christ-like,* requires *real honesty,*
true humility, *charity* and a *right* understanding of
self, that that self may be *rightly used* in *all* the concerns of life, temporal and spiritual.

5

There *may* be, as there often is, a *vast* difference between a PROFESSED Christian and an *honest* man, who goes humbly and unostentatiously along through life, bestrewing his pathway with kind *acts, charitable deeds*, and noble examples of purity and uprightness. True, such a man does not generally gain the clamor and applause of the multitude, because *not* working in the harness of *popular sentiment* and religious routine, but he gains that which is infinitely better—a good culture and growth of self, becomes *individualized*, which is the highest aim of man, receives the blessings of poor and honest souls, and, if there be an inheritance beyond the grave of bones, its immortal boon.

To be pure-minded, noble and aspirational, to grow and expand into fulness of *individual* growth, possessed of qualities which make man what he should be, reasonable, decided, humane, charitable, honest, moral, and religious, is to be *natural*, observing nature's *laws*, and pruning self thereby with honest endeavor. Man has all he can justly do in weeding and pruning his own garden and vine. It is *his*, and for *him* to cultivate; none other can do it for him, neither can he rightly care for his own, if engaged in attending to those of others. *Self* is his portion in life to prune, and he must nourish that self rightly, by giving it proper care and food, and thus *out*grow its *in*herent properties into ripeness, to the expansion and ripening of which there is no end, if but the right way and means for doing so are understood. From the acorn *out*grows the staunch and majestic oak, so

man, by bringing *out* what is *in* him, growing it, enlarging and perfecting it, becomes the strong, high-
minded, noble, dignified man, truly learned and wise.
Man *cannot* cultivate the *natural powers* greatly by
any process of *in*stuffing of other people's ideas, the
outgrowth of *their* brains, but must *out*grow his *own*,
by studying the laws of *his* being, the mechanism of
his own machinery, and moving it in accordance
therewith. Here lies the *great* secret of *greatness*, viz.:
to rely upon the *natural* powers within *self*, and *out*-
grow them ; thus enlarging and ripening the brain
into a perfected instrument for the reception of
thought. An organ of the brain cannot act with
power, any more than a muscle, until it is *developed*
by *use*, therefore *think*, oh, man! grow *self*, train *all*
your faculties, the spiritual equally with the rest,
place all under the guidance of your own *reason*, and
become a MAN! a *true, dignified, noble man ;* and
when you have grown *self*, you will find that self
equal to all its own needs, knowing *how* to *truly live,
truly worship*, and to be truly good, fulfilling the
simple *divinely* imposed duty of being an *honest* and
natural man.

A few words more before I close this chapter, in
relation to the churches. As I look abroad, over our
land, and note the *costly* houses of worship, which
rear their tall spires heavenward in every city, involv-
ing millions and millions of dollars in their erection
and maintenance, I ask myself how much this great
fund, used with the yearly efforts which now accumu-
lates it in the church, might do toward relieving the

suffering poor of our country? Instead of taking from
the poor man's labor his mite of hard-earned means,
and putting it within the coffers of church, how much
better would it be to distribute it among the poor
with the same zeal and energy that is now put forth
to gather and hoard it up in costly church edifices!
How much more *humane* and *Christ-like!* and how
much more noble the *act*, and elevating. Would not
worship be quite as acceptable to the Almighty if it
were less showy, and given in less costly houses?

Ah! fortunate, indeed, it is for the *modern church*
and *prevailing Christianity*, that Christ does not live
to-day in *America*. Methinks he would consider it
somewhat different from preaching by the *wayside*,
and to *all people*, out in the fields, groves, temples of
nature, where the incense of heaven baptizes all alike,
and the inspiration of sweet nature lifts the soul in
humble admiration and reverence to a just God, who
has made all this *beautiful* creation, and placed man
therein, to live according to the laws of reciprocal
unity, in peace, prosperity and happiness—a humble,
charitable, moral and *natural* being, filled with that
love towards his fellow-men which God gives to all.

CHAPTER V.

PHYSICAL SLAVERY.

ENORMOUS as is the evil of physical slavery, which has been for so long a time, and still is an encumbrance upon our fair land, yet it is of small consequence compared to that *mental* slavery of which I have treated in preceding chapters, and of which *physical slavery* is one of the *results*. I say that mental slavery is much the worst, because *out* of *it* grows the many physical evils in our midst, which only being seen by superficial observers, are deemed the *entire* wrong, while really they are the effects of deeper causes, and those causes *mental darkness* and *ignorance*. Evils, such as I speak of, vanish rapidly before *true enlightenment* and civilization, because, being the effects of wrong mental culture and ignorance, they disappear just in proportion as the causes are removed, and light and knowledge take the place of ignorance and superstition; therefore, I repeat, that Mental Slavery is a far more deplorable state of bondage than mere physical servitude.

For further proof of my assertion, there is the *fact*, that intelligent and enlightened people cannot be held in physical bondage, but only the undeveloped and ignorant. And so it is *mentally;* only the uneducated and undeveloped *spiritually*, can be held in mental subjection to superstitious dogmas and false doctrines, that the few priestly men may hold power over them, and thus perpetuate a religious aristocracy, the same exactly as the few slaveholders, physically keep power over the masses of slaves, and through their labor, on means that cost them no *wages*, DONATED to them, build up and maintain an aristocracy in living. The two systems of slavery produce the same results—*worldly* power and aristocracy—which could not be otherwise, since they are so nearly allied; one being the legitimate or natural effect of the other. Both hold sway for worldly aggrandizement and power, and both in violation of higher law and principle; one much more grave and evil than the other, however, because *professing* to deal with spiritual things, and teach spiritual enlightenment; while really it benights the mind, and confines, instead of expands, the *interior* spiritual perceptions, fitting men to become the perpetrators of all kinds of evil, *as* the *natural* result of their *want* of *real, true,* SPIRITUAL *knowledge*, having which, they would be noble, truthful, pure men.

Thus we see that teaching men, who are their own masters *physically*, wrong spiritual instructions, and keeping their minds in ignorance of the beautiful laws and truths of nature, of philosophy, and of science, which is true civilization, gives to the world an element of vast mischief, because such men are free to act out the promptings of their education, while the African, held in physical and mental bondage too, is *not free* to contaminate the world, and therefore his power for executing the evils his situation might prompt, is vastly inferior to the freeman's, while *naturally*, too, he is greatly inferior in development, and consequently in power for wrong-doing. The simple holding, then, of the poor, half-developed, uneducated African in bondage, constitutes, when weighed by higher law, a crime in importance quite insignificant to that mental slavery which makes of the stalwart sons and fair daughters of America mental dwarfs, and puny butterflies of fashion, by degrading the spiritual understanding, stinting and stultifying their God-given faculties, planting error, superstition, and artifice in the stead of *truth*, love, and wisdom.

The nation, with its war and turmoil, is fast uprooting *physical* bondage and giving freedom to the slave. Northern sentiment, based more upon *principle* and *justice* than the Southern, would not allow the unlimited wide-spread of the nefarious schemes of the South, and therefore she began "kicking against the pricks" of stern *opposition*, little thinking, in her short-sightedness, that she was stirring up the elements of right and wrong into such antagonism as should prove the downfall of her long-cherished institution of slavery; yet so it is. And not only so, but arousing the latent principles of justice throughout the whole country to such an extent, that all the long existing *causes* of evil, which have been and are insidiously working to man's retardation of progress *spiritually*, will soon be swept with the ruins of physical slavery into the forgotten past: false doctrines and theories, error and superstition must give way before the swift advancing tide of true civilization and enlightenment, which *this* age, the age of *reason* and *insight*, is unfolding. The eternal principles of right and justice are coming uppermost, and before the light of divine *truth* all wrong and falsity must pale, swept with the ruins and dust of ages into oblivion, by the "bright shining light" of *spiritual science.*

Back of all the apparent wrongs in the land are deep-hidden *causes*, which pervade all conditions of society, and *revolution* will not stop the turning of her mighty wheel until we stand as a nation purified from our sins, the measure of which is the penalty we pay. Root and branch must the monster tree of slavery in all its forms be pulled out of the national heart, to do which we have commenced at the top, chopping off its branches,—physical bondage,—and unless we continue until its very roots are extracted, it will sprout again, firmer and deeper-rooted than before, for *future* generations to battle with. *Now* is the time to strike sturdy blows for our national honor, if we would plant a republic upon the God-given principles of truth, justice, and *liberty.*

This question of African slavery has been agitated and discussed almost unlimitedly to prove its justice or injustice, and whether it be *constitutional* or not. In a preceding chapter I have endeavored to show the proper relation of the terms freedom and slavery by the mutual or reciprocal relations of all things, commencing with universal laws as regulating the astro nomical bodies, and observing *their* mutual relations according to law divine, showing this law to extend to *man* as to every thing else; therefore, weighed by the higher law moral, law of universal reciprocity established by Divinity, there can be no hesitancy in answering the questions whether slavery be right or wrong, and whether *justly constitutional.*

If the science of nature, the laws of its life and its philosophy, speak any teachings to man, they are those of a higher power, and which man cannot justly set aside for inventions of his own; and looking at life in all its phases metaphysically, scientifically, and reasonably, we read lessons which unmistakably pronounce a judgment upon *all* systems of slavery, and denounce them as *evil.* Nowhere in the vast arena of the natural and beautiful, whose author and sustainer is the Omnipotent, Omniscient, and Omnipresent Power, can man find lessons of evil, or read any laws upholding slavery in any form, save those of reciprocal unity.

Nature is all equally an aristocracy, with no false pride like that of man; she is true to her development, real and stable. In no unfolding of the natural world is there any slavery and aristocracy, save with man: he invents it in many forms to impose upon his brother man, for wealth and power to gratify his *animal* passions.

There .can be but *one* source of reference to determine the right or wrong of slavery, and that is *divine justice*, as seen in the one universal law manifest in all natural phenomena,—the law of *reciprocity*. In other words, there is a positive and negative power in nature which keep an equilibrium, a just balance by their *mutual* blendings. To illustrate: there cannot be an *all*-positive power regardless of and usurping

5*

every thing else within itself; for instance, the sun is positive to the lesser orbs that revolve about it, but *not* all-positive, else it would swallow up, consume, so to speak, all the others : on the contrary, however, the law mutual is perfect, and the power exerted by the sun fully reciprocated *by* the others, keeping beautiful harmony among the heavenly bodies. So in all the concerns of a world, there is this law of mutuality, regulating all its productions, from the mineral up to *man*, where alone is violation. Man *only* disregards the divine law of control in his earth career, and upon short-sighted worldly schemes, fills himself with temporal power for a time at the sacrifice of *principle*, to satisfy the cravings of an abnormal *pride*, and then explodes into ruin, as the South is now doing with its system of negro slavery.

For many generations has the aristocratic portion of the South flourished grandly upon a system of labor which has cost them *no wages*, but the law of reciprocal justice has been hanging over them all the time, and at last the blow has come; all the inhuman wrongs of Satanic men are being wiped out with terrible vengeance, and the lordly aristocracy of slave-holders reduced to a condition inferior even to that of the slave, for the poor African, although deprived of his own native freedom and peculiar modes of living, is actually benefited by contact and *amalgamation* with the white master, while the master now sinks into bankruptcy and worldly ruin, to say nothing of his *moral* degradation. Thus the law divine of *mutuality* stands as forcibly just in regard to man, as to all other things, and, though disregarded for years, or centuries even, finally makes its rightful and stern demands felt and answered. Man ·holds reciprocal relations to his fellow-men, or relations of *positive* and *negative interest*, and whatever his plane of development, as much is *exacted* as is given : he gains his all of life from nature, and if he stands *high* in the scale of unfoldment, his duty is none the less imperative to give to the world as much as is received therefrom ; that is, if he be enlightened his light must be bright and shining, and his acts elevating, not *binding* down, for if he use his superior knowledge and power as *means* to crush out and trample upon the rights of his weaker brother, he shall surely in turn be crushed, for the *law* is *just* and *inevitable*.

What if man disregard *justice*, court mammon, and thrive largely for a lifetime even, what profiteth it him ? He cannot lug his worldly gains into eternity, but instead, carries the *curses* they entail, and in the *next life* pays the penalty of his wrong-doing *by taking* the place his *acts*, and consequent development, fit ·him to occupy—a philosophy and religion which teach man to be good.

The condition of the enslaved and the enslaving is not one of reciprocity, of *mutual* benefit, but enriches one in worldly good at the sacrifice of the other's bodily comfort and mental liberty, or ownership : the *law* is *not* respected, and the natural results must follow, as they *now* are doing. There are no just reciprocal relations between master and slave, no *principle* of *unity* binding them together, but instead

coercion, one losing all his rights, while the other
gains them and is proportionately enriched; one loses
his own native freedom, and sacrifices life in hard toil
to satisfy the other's selfish ambition.   Looks this
like justness, like principle, like reciprocity and humanity, like morality, equity and religion ?   Yet how
many arguments have been deduced from that book
called Bible, to uphold African slavery, and thus perpetuate an institution in which *all* the above-named
qualities are wholly wanting.   And taking the Bible
as *authority*, the arguments from it are very strong
in favor of slavery, and naturally enough since the
whole object in the compilation and manufacture of
the Bible, is the enslavement of the mental, for pre-
cisely the same ends as physical enslavement, viz. :
wealth, power, aristocracy and *leisure*.

This same system of mental, or religious slavery
is indirectly the cause of so much ignorance and poverty in the world, because it teaches a system of ethics,
which carried out in social and business life results
in the infernal monopolies, speculations, and dishon
esties, that now enrich the few far beyond their needs,
and leave the million slaves to poverty, many actually
starving; for does not popular Christianity teach doctrines of election, one-side-ism, that *they* are better
than others? and are they not going to monopolize
all of God's beautiful heaven to themselves *exclusively*, while they consign all the rest—about thirteen-
fourteenths—to eternal torment, because they are *not
like them?*   Is not my assertion true ?   Are not the
proofs of it apparent everywhere throughout society ?

Where is found the most church influence, is not there also found the most slavery to fashion, *pride*, and wealth?

I say, that teaching which produces mental slavery is the cause of all physical bondage, because it teaches *falsehood* for spiritual truths, and gives to the human understanding really no enlightenment in regard to the real and beautiful truths of its nature; does not open the fount of life to man through *philosophy* and *reason*, but rather blinds and stints his *natural* perceptions, and therefore turns him into channels of thought and business which are in accordance with his early inculcations—his education. That teaching which shows a man his real and *true* position in life, which unravels the metaphysics of his own existence, revealing to him the beautiful and wise laws of his own being, makes him a good man. Other than this depraves him, for that is depravity which departs from divine instructions.

Man cannot substitute his own nefarious schemes, devoid of *principle*, in the stead of the beautiful, progressive, harmonious, and wise laws of the Eternal, and be *good*, nor long flourish.

There are *principles* of life as intimately woven into our existence as life itself, and those principles are the *inevitable laws* of being, which cannot be overthrown.

Nations come to wars as the natural results of man's disobedience to divine law, *not* from divine design. The turmoils of man are only the elements immediately connected with him, upheaving and conflicting with divine justice because of his disobedience, and each time they do thus, divine justice rules with more power—reform is more complete. Ideas that are *worldly*, unholy, impure and unjust, are acted upon and embodied into institutions, which institutions, not having a right basis, soon work their own ruin, because, forsooth, *divine* rule is stronger than man's. These ideas are generally inculcated in the early religious training of the child, and carried out into *action* as it grows into manhood. Thus it is with physical slavery: back in the religious training, and consequent aristocracy of the *old world*, were engendered the ideas which gave rise to American Slavery, and through the religious teachings and ecclesiastical power which has underlain the education of the American People, has it been perpetuated, until *now* the ruin it has worked for itself is at hand.

Wrong, I repeat, is the result of ignorance—ignorance of principle, of science, philosophy, truth—and ignorance is the result of that system of education and religious training which teach avarice, selfishness, uncharitableness, *special favors* and vicarious atonement, election and one-side-ism, eternal damnation and special salvation, and many base notions, *base* because UNTRUTHFUL. It is all this that has supported physical slavery in our fair land and upon our fertile soil for so long a time, a land called *free*, and a nation shouting *liberty!* But thanks to the powers ruling, the stain is fast being wiped out, the disgrace cast into oblivion, and the *causes* probed to their centre: the axe is being laid at the *root* of the tree, and old theology and superstition outrooted from their strongholds. With the cessation of hostilities in the field will come the warring of the political, social, and religious elements of society; in fact they are already jarring and working, and the principles of divine justice and truth, like the leaven in the meal, at work leavening the whole. *Right* must prevail and reforms come, reforms in habits of living, dress, business, thinking and acting, else the American People will soon dwindle into complete physical degeneracy, from disregard of the simple, healthful laws of life.

What gain is it, I ask, to waste a whole lifetime in pursuit of the almighty dollar? To enjoy the good and beautiful in life, we must first *culture self* to an appreciating capacity, which is *better* than great riches. The mere matter of wealth does not bring culture, and *without* culture there is little enjoyment; I mean *right* culture, culture *naturally*, spending more time in studying to embellish the brain with golden thoughts, than the pocket with golden dollars. A man may have all the wealth in the world, and *without* culture of self is still an ignoramus, not capable of half the enjoyment as the poor man by his side. It is what we get *out* of *our own heads* by culture, that makes us truly rich, not what we get into our pockets. Money is good rightly used, but brains are better.

There are the best of reasons, other than that of taking what does not belong to one out of the general fund, why a man should not labor so hard to become rich. Supposing, as I have said in a preceding chapter, that there should be equality in the distribution of worldly goods, is it not plain that every man would have plenty with moderate effort? And instead of spending all his time in hard toil to compete with a *selfish* world, wearing life out not only thus–– but giving to himself a one-idea culture, he would have plenty of time for *self-study*, for expanding and enriching his *interior* nature by giving it general care, and enjoying his life to the full capacity. Then he would have that self-satisfied, complacent happiness which a true culture gives, whereas now he knows of no enjoyment save in the superficial world, through his money, and that is never fully satisfying, but leaves a restless, haggard, and dissatisfied feeling, which is not elevating but rather wearing upon life : a species of dissipation that is now so rapidly sapping out the healthy life-currents of the nation.

Honest toil is *true worship ;* worship of *principle, justice* and *truth.* *Dishonest* or *selfish* toil is worship of devil, mammon, pride and passion. If mankind lived rightly they would not need such extensive trades, gigantic business operations, costly houses, and so forth, to satisfy their morbid ambition. Simplicity, beauty, order, harmony and justice are the *divine* attributes of man.

Physical slavery comes in as a *means* to satisfy his selfish desires, to gratify an abnormal *pride*, and give a little worldly power for a time, but it is damning to the white man to thus gain his wealth, demoralizing and degrading to his better nature, his spiritual interests and enlightenment, because in direct opposition to true spiritual teaching ; while the negro is perhaps

actually benefited; certainly contact and association
with the more civilized world is a benefit to him,
though that benefit at the expense of his *freedom*, is
doubtfil. By *amalgamation*, however, is slavery a very
great benefit to the *black* man, but that is an *unnatu-
ral* mode of civilization : in his own tropical barbarity
is his *native* element, in which are all the refinements
necessary to his degree of development. Every thing
in the world has *its* proper sphere to fill and mission
to work out in the grand scheme of creation, civilization, and progress, and the African has his. America,
with her abundant resources, knowledge, and superior
civilization, can do much towards the enlightenment
of ignorant, barbaric nations in whatever part of the
globe, but not properly so by *enslaving* them, for that
cannot be done without disastrous consequences to the
enslaving party, because transgressing divine law, the
law reciprocal, the law just, and law *truth*. Slavery
to the African is not *charity* towards him, but selfish
monopoly *of* him, and though there may result partial
civilization to him in consequence, yet it makes the
transgression of the law none the less evil, for like the
tendency of heat and cold to blend until there is a
mean between the two *extremes*, so it is with human
beings; the force of circumstances does much towards
elevating or depressing them, for the tendency in
their social and business relations is that of heat and
cold—to blend. If a man habitually deal or associate with his inferiors from choice or interest, he is
lessened just in proportion as they are raised. Such
is the law, which is fully illustrated in the deprav-

ity of Southern morals, devoid almost entirely of *principle*.

Man cannot associate with wicked associates without gradually becoming like them, so a man cannot deal in physical slavery without crushing out the finer and higher principles of his nature, because he applies his talent to the control and perpetuating of an institution which is immoral and unjust, and therefore *degrading* to himself : instead of aspiring to do *good*, dealing with others according to just laws and precepts, he disobeys the *right*, and is proportionately debased, retarded in growth and spiritual advancement.

Physical Slavery, therefore, is not so great an evil to the slave as to the master ; the utter disregard of principle it maintains is more disastrous to the white man, than is *bondage* to the black ; for the American slave owner is *enlightened*, and the *sole agent* in this total disregard of *right*, while the slave is *not* a voluntary agent in the perpetuation of the system, there fore the whole responsibility rests with the master, and the penalties incurred in carrying on a wicked institution he must answer for. What benefit may arise to the slave is wholly unintentional with the master, and constitutes *no part* of the *object* he has in holding slaves, so that *morally* he is *not* to have the credit of doing any good to the black man, because *not* his *intention*, therefore the plea which has been so often made in favor of slavery, that the benefit to the black man justifies it, is no plea at all, since the only object in holding slaves is for gain to gratify *selfish* feelings, and *not* to do the slave a *benefit*.

The more that can be whipped and ground out of him the better, is the *principle* (!) acted upon; aristocratic laziness the aim sought, an aristocracy which has its sympathy among the aristocrats North, by many ties of intermarriages, intertrades, and reciprocal interests of various kinds, and now that the South, with its *peculiar system*, rebels against the government, may be seen the Northern sympathizers showing their interests in Southern behalf. Aristocracies are sympathetic the world over. The church aristocracy, wealth aristocracy, and slave aristocracy, are all based upon the same selfish, worldly, unrighteous aims, and all having one and the same object—*power*.

But there is to be a reign of *principle;* the age of *reason* begins to see the *right*, and old aristocracy, with all its varied monopoly, must tumble; its basis is unjust, and the advance march of *truth* will level it with the dust. All its base notions and false teachings the world will soon be emancipated from, by the inception of knowledge, truth, and justice. The shackles of all bondage will fall off as the light of *true* civilization and religion advances. Old theology and superstition stand to-day quaking in their strongholds, for they begin to see through the gathering gloom, the rays of *true spiritual light*, which will penetrate their mysteries and dissolve and destroy their power. They know it is only a question of *time*, for as the *masses* progress in knowledge, just in that ratio is ecclesiastical influence gone, and the institutions it gives rise to laid low.

The march of true civilization has commenced, and

the great civil war which *now* agitates our fair land but the infinite powers striking blows for *liberty.* *Emancipation* is the war-cry, and the reform now begun will not cease until a new era is established, and that era one of spiritual insight, of principle, truth, and justice, of reason, philosophy, and wisdom, and of *freedom* from all bigotry, narrow-mindedness, superstition, and slavish notions.

The decree has gone forth: The Emancipation proclamation of the Almighty is issued, and the work will be done, and *well* done. Already the soldiers of *Right,* clad in the armor of *Truth,* stand around thick, ready to rush at the war-cry: with their glittering bayonets of eternal steel, will they pierce the heart of old superstition, and banish *ignorance, selfishness,* and *old-fogyism,* with *knowledge, love,* and *wisdom. Reason,* the dictator of the human *will* has raised its voice for *justice,* and methinks I see marshalled upon the plains of invisible life, the hosts of the "mighty dead," ready to strike in Reason's cause, and help place liberated humanity upon planes of more elevated, dignified, noble man and womanhood.

The tocsin of the Infinite has sounded the alarum, the war-cry, is heard, the march is *forward,* and the instigators, perpetrators, and perpetuators of *human enslavement* cannot flee from the wrath to come. Stern Justice, with its law reciprocal, stands ready to administer meet reward; to each wrong *its penalty* until *all* are atoned for. *Law infinite* cannot be evaded; it offers *every thing,* and exacts full obedience.

CHAPTER VI.

EPILOGUE TO AMERICA.

ACTION is always preceded by an idea necessarily; *action* is the *execution* of an idea. If the *idea* be wrong the *action* is wrong, and therefore the result is also wrong; consequently all the evils which beset communities and nations, are the effects of wrong ideas *executed*. Ideas are *right* or *wrong* in proportion as they embody *divine principles*. There is no standard of right but the divine, and in just so much as man learns and heeds that, in so far is he wise. Nations are made up of individuals, and in proportion as individuals are wise, so will be the nation, therefore the national authority should be directed to the right culture of the *individual*, seeing to it, that institutions for education, intellectually and morally, are based upon *divine principles*.

Governmental execution has been to conceive and carry out wrong ideas in the *past*, in some particulars of national policy, consequently we have in America to-day a powerful civil war, the *result* of *acting* from *wrong ideas :* the *effect* has been true to the *cause*, and civil war, in all its horrid aspects, is but the warring of those wrong *ideas* with *principles*, and which will not cease in secure peace until the *cause* is antidoted by *effect ;* when, if the nation's actions for the *future*, be based upon ideas of justice and right, there will be lasting peace and prosperity, but should she again act unwisely, should she act upon *ideas antagonistic* to *principle*, the *result* of such wrong action will again be manifest, sooner or later, in national war and turmoil.

Nations like individuals cannot act wrong without paying the penalty.

The Constitution of the United States embodies wrong ideas, ideas devoid of justice, and therefore has it failed to conduct the nation, in its unparalleled pro gress, *safely* onward, until not a century has she sailed thus rapidly on over the great sea of Time, before we see her shattered into fragments, and her Constitution, in many of its particulars, a dead letter, which man can never patch up, and by which she can never again steer her course upon the great chart of life.

The emergencies of the times have stricken forever from its pages the damnable clauses, that have launched us upon so troubled a sea, the waters of which will not be still at the commanding. A *new* constitution, embodying *Principles* instead of wrong ideas, shall henceforth guide the "helm of state," and again will she sail on smooth seas of peace and progress, a "Union strong and great," bidding defiance to all the jarring elements and discords of the old world.

ITELLECTUAL FREEDOM;

OR,

EMANCIPATION

FROM

MENTAL AND PHYSICAL BONDAGE.

/BY

CHARLES S. WOODRUFF, M. D.,

AUTHOR OF "LEGALIZED PROSTITUTION," ETC.

SINCLAIR TOUSEY,

121 NASSAU STREET, N. Y.,

AGENT FOR THE AUTHOR.